# SHOCK & AWE

A SIDEWINDER STORY

ABIGAIL ROUX

Riptide Publishing
PO Box 6652
Hillsborough, NJ 08844
www.riptidepublishing.com

This is a work of fiction. Names, characters, places, and incidents are either the product of the author's imagination or are used fictitiously. Any resemblance to actual persons living or dead, business establishments, events, or locales is entirely coincidental.

Shock & Awe (A Sidewinder Story)
Copyright © 2013 by Abigail Roux

Cover Art by L.C. Chase, lcchase.com/design.htm
Editor: Rachel Haimowitz
Layout: L.C. Chase, lcchase.com/design.htm

All rights reserved. No part of this book may be reproduced or transmitted in any form or by any means, electronic or mechanical, including photocopying, recording, or by any information storage and retrieval system without the written permission of the publisher, and where permitted by law. Reviewers may quote brief passages in a review. To request permission and all other inquiries, contact Riptide Publishing at the mailing address above, at Riptidepublishing.com, or at marketing@riptidepublishing.com.

ISBN: 978-1-62649-056-7

First edition
November, 2013

Also available in ebook:
ISBN: 978-1-62649-055-0

# SHOCK & AWE

## A SIDEWINDER STORY

ABIGAIL ROUX

# TABLE OF CONTENTS

Kelly had to lean against the railing of his front porch while Nick dealt with the lock and the alarm to his cabin. He pressed his hand to his chest, resting his palm over the healing bullet wound just under his left pectoral. It had been a long plane ride, even in first class, and the hour-long trip from the airport hadn't been much better on him. He was exhausted, and all he wanted was his own bed.

Nick left the luggage at the door and hustled inside to turn off the beeping alarm. Kelly didn't have to tell him the code. They all knew where the keys to their castles were: Ty's and Owen's security codes, Nick's yacht, and a mental map of Digger's bayou booby traps.

The beeping from inside stopped, and Nick returned to roll the luggage out of the way. Kelly wrapped his arm over Nick's shoulders, and they hobbled through the front door. He could walk on his own when they'd left the hospital in New Orleans, but after so much travel, he wasn't actually sure he could anymore.

"Thanks for doing this, bud," Kelly muttered.

"Hey," Nick grunted. "We both know you took that bullet for me. Least I can do is get you home."

Kelly didn't argue. He couldn't claim he'd taken the bullet on purpose, but if he hadn't been there, it would have lodged in Nick's head, and they both knew how that would have ended. He leaned on Nick until they reached the worn leather recliner in the living room, but he hesitated as Nick tried to help lower him into it.

"What's wrong?"

Kelly laughed. "I'm not sure I'll be able to get out of this thing if I get down."

"It's not like you're going anywhere." Nick tightened his grip on Kelly's waist and eased him into the recliner. "And I'm not carrying your ass upstairs right now, so sit."

"You're a horrible nursemaid."

Nick pulled the handle on the side of the chair and shot Kelly's legs out.

As soon as the chair stopped wobbling, Kelly closed his eyes and relaxed into its familiar folds. He listened to Nick banging around, bringing their luggage inside, going through the refrigerator. Nick gasped and closed the refrigerator door quickly. They'd been gone a long time; Kelly had no doubt what the inside of that thing smelled like.

Nick finally came back into the living room with a glass of water. "You ready for meds? I'm going to put you to sleep and go get some groceries. And . . . maybe some rubber gloves."

Kelly mustered a smile. "Sounds good."

Nick tapped one of the painkillers into his palm and grinned. "Bank shot?"

Kelly opened his mouth, and Nick tossed a pill into it, then another, snickering as he handed Kelly the glass of water. He threw a blanket over him, put the television remote and his cell phone within reach, then patted Kelly's head.

"I'll be back before you wake up."

Kelly closed his eyes, relaxing so the pills could to do their work. He knew he didn't have anything to worry about as long as Nick was on the job.

When Kelly awoke, it was to the sound of humming and the smell of bacon frying and a hint of Lysol. It took him a moment to remember where he was and why he was sore. He stared at Nick, who was curled on the couch a few feet away with a book.

"Hey," he said, his voice hoarse.

Nick jerked, glancing up at him. He set his book aside and scooted forward, but he didn't stand. "You okay? Need more pills?"

"No, I'm good. What's that sound?"

Nick went still and listened briefly, then shook his head. "I don't hear anything."

Kelly held his breath and realized the humming sound had faded. So had the smell. "Are you cooking bacon?"

Nick began to chuckle, then fought hard to stop. "No. Do you want me to be?"

"No. Yeah. Wait, no, no."

Nick waited patiently, still smiling.

Kelly just stared at him, trying to get his brain to work. He wasn't sure if he was hallucinating, if his brain had picked up on all the things Nick had been doing while he'd slept and then replayed them to him, or if he was just losing his mind. He wasn't sure he cared, though, because now that he was fully awake, he was in pain again. "Okay, I need another pill," he finally said. Nick reached for the pill bottle. "But half of it this time. I'm tired of you laughing at me for being drugged."

Nick merely nodded as he fished a pill out. He broke it and popped one half into his mouth before handing the other to Kelly.

"What the hell, O'Flaherty?" Kelly asked, laughing despite how much it hurt to do so.

"Consider it payment for services rendered," Nick said as he took a sip of Kelly's water. Kelly gaped. Nick laughed harder and handed Kelly a whole pill to add to the half. "It's like a step above Tylenol, don't hurt yourself."

Kelly was still chuckling while he tried to down the painkillers.

"You think you're going to be more comfortable here or in your bed tonight?"

Kelly peered at the darkened windows. He dreaded nighttime, because that was when he hurt more and slept fitfully. There was never anything on TV to entertain him in the wee hours when he was wide awake, and he'd sped through all the books he had access to. It also got lonely, because he wasn't about to keep Nick awake at night as well as depend on him during the day. "Is it that time already?"

Nick shrugged. "Close enough."

"Well. If I sleep here, you can have my bed."

"Doc, if you sleep here I'll be on the couch in case you need me. If you sleep upstairs, I'll make a pallet on the floor."

"Promise not to roll in your sleep, and I'll share the bed."

Nick gave him an easy smile and stood. "Worth a try. I've promised more for a bed."

"You whore," Kelly said, grinning as he slid his arm around Nick's neck and held tight for Nick to help him stand.

Once he was out of the recliner, he shuffled off to the bathroom on the ground floor. He could hear Nick lugging the suitcases up the steps to the loft bedroom of the cabin. Kelly was beyond grateful Nick had insisted he come with Kelly until he was well enough to fend for himself. Otherwise he didn't like to think where he'd be stuck, or who would be stuck taking care of him. Nick was using every last hour of vacation time the Boston PD gave him to be here.

It took them a full five minutes to get Kelly up the stairs, mostly because they had to keep stopping to laugh at the absurdity of it, and by the time he eased onto the edge of his bed, they were both out of breath.

Kelly looked up at Nick and grinned. "Bet you never worked this hard to get a guy in bed, have you?"

"Not physically, no," Nick grunted. He pulled back the covers and arranged the pillows for support, then Kelly wrapped an arm around his neck and Nick leaned over him as he eased him into the bed.

Kelly had to squeeze his eyes closed against the pull. It wasn't really pain anymore, but there was some serious discomfort when he twisted and stretched, and the muscles were weak. Anything that forced him to use his core was still too much for him. He had to be careful or stitches and staples would tear loose.

Nick was still hovering over him when he opened his eyes. "You okay?"

"Yeah," Kelly gasped. He cleared his throat. "That might not have been worth the effort."

Nick grinned crookedly. "Well that's the first time I've heard *that* before."

Kelly made a derogatory sound and closed his eyes again. Nick pulled away, then gently covered him with the sheet.

Kelly may have been the corpsman, but Nick had always been the caretaker of the group. He'd been a wingman, fall guy, sounding board, and alibi. He'd been mother, father, big brother, and crazy uncle. Whatever they'd needed. He'd always been the one who'd made sure all the Sidewinder ducks were in a row, and he was probably the sole reason the house they'd all shared in Jacksonville hadn't burned down.

It was so odd to think back on all those years and know that Nick had been hiding part of himself he thought he couldn't share. It almost broke Kelly's heart to think of all the secrets he'd spilled to Nick, all the things he'd gotten off his chest, but Nick had never been able to do the same.

Kelly opened his eyes to watch Nick. He was dragging Kelly's suitcase toward the armoire. "How'd you make the jump, anyway?" Kelly asked. He had to close his eyes again as exhaustion threatened.

"What jump?"

"I mean, were you always into guys and just hid it? Were all the girls we chased together just a cover, or . . ."

"No," Nick said quickly. Kelly opened one eye to see Nick clearing off the table beside the bed. He was smirking as he spoke. "I consider myself equal opportunity."

Kelly watched him curiously. Over the years, Kelly had seen Nick's charisma and easy manner pull more barroom trysts than Ty and Digger combined. Sometimes it almost seemed like he did it by accident. Of course, that was all part of Nick's charm. A lot of what he did seemed accidental, which had contributed to other Marines calling him Lucky for much of his career. But Kelly knew better. Nick's methods were very deliberate, and his results were anything but luck.

Nick was a fascinating person, and Kelly had always thought so. When he'd first joined the team, Ty and Nick had been quite intimidating. Fiercely loyal to each other, dangerously protective of each other, and so close they could finish each other's sentences and communicate without words. Once Kelly had proven himself worthy, he'd been afforded the same loyalty from both men. With Ty, it was like being surrounded by a barricade of barbed wire and mines. Nick's loyalty felt more like being wrapped in a warm blanket. Everything about Nick felt warm, even the thought of him, and ever since Nick had come out to him, Kelly had wondered what that meant for *him*.

What did it mean that Kelly knew he would choose Nick over anyone else if a gun was put to his head? What did it mean that Nick's calls or texts always left him feeling both happy and melancholy all at the same time? What did it mean when his heart dropped into his toes as he'd listened to Nick confess that he'd been in love with Ty for over a decade?

Even now the thought sent a pang through his chest that made his wound throb and ache. He placed his hand over it.

"What's it like?" he asked suddenly.

Nick glanced over at him as he slid the lamp away from the bed and laid out Kelly's pill bottles, bandages, and other necessities. "What's what like?"

"Being with a guy." He looked Nick up and down, trying to imagine. Would Nick be the same with a man as he was with a woman? Because Kelly had seen that, and it had looked fun. "Is it different?"

Nick shrugged and nodded. "Sort of, yeah. Physically? Definitely. Relationships, though, it depends a lot on who you're with." He glanced at Kelly and raised an eyebrow, smiling. "You a little bi-curious, Doc?"

Kelly laughed again, holding his side in a wasted attempt to keep it from hurting. "I don't know."

"You don't know?" Nick teased. "Either you're curious or you're not."

"I guess. I mean, I like sex."

"Granted," Nick mumbled, still smiling.

"I never thought about it before." That was a damn lie. "But hell, if you can do it, so can I, right?"

Nick placed his hand on Kelly's forehead, holding it there briefly before patting him and then moving away. He headed for the bathroom, probably making sure the path from Kelly's side of the bed was clear.

"And a beautiful person is a beautiful person, so why not open up that door to more opportunities?" Kelly called after him, desperate to have him return so they could continue the conversation.

"I think you're omnivorous," Nick said, his voice echoing off the tile and into the bedroom.

Kelly laughed again. He rested back to watch Nick move around the room. He was like a mother hen, prepping the nest. He moved the chair from the corner to the middle of the room, a convenient place for Kelly to get to and rest if he needed to. He went to the armoire beside the bathroom door and pulled out several extra pillows, putting pillowcases on them and tossing them on the bed. He was going to use them as a barrier between himself and Kelly as they slept, to protect Kelly's wound from any stray limbs.

Kelly found himself wishing those pillows wouldn't be there tonight. He didn't know why. Painkillers? Knowing Nick was bi and having the nerve to ask questions? Watching Ty and Zane and the connection they obviously shared while in New Orleans? Kelly had never felt that with his ex-wife, not once, but he'd certainly felt it with brothers-in-arms. Maybe it was a perfect storm of factors, but Kelly was definitely curious. Asking Nick these questions had given him a little rush too. *Nick* gave him a little rush.

He had always been closest to Nick. Nick had been Kelly's best man at his wedding. He'd also been the one who'd taken him in briefly after he'd divorced. They were very much alike in temperament, compared to the others who were all fire and stone. He and Nick were water and smoke: patient and nebulous and easy.

"I'm going to take a shower," Nick said as he threw the last spare pillow on the bed. "You want anything from downstairs first?"

Kelly's breath quickened, and he blurted it out before he could think twice. "Why Ty?"

Nick stopped short and cocked his head as if he hadn't heard right. "What?"

"When you came out to me, you told me you'd been in love with Ty," Kelly explained. He held his breath, telling himself the answer would probably make his wound throb again and he didn't really want to know. "Why Ty?"

Nick blushed and lowered his head, chewing on his lip. He shrugged. "He was . . . like this big shining beacon. For a long time I was a little in love with the idea of him. The idea of that kind of loyalty and trust for the rest of your life, you know? I think it was mostly just being young and wanting to believe in something. You know Ty. He was easy to believe in."

Kelly nodded. "Are you still in love with him?"

Nick was already shaking his head. He came around the other side of the bed and sat, leaning against the headboard so Kelly couldn't see his face without twisting. "We went through too much. Nothing romantic about it. And the night I kissed him, the night I told you about everything, there was nothing there. We would have worked if we'd wanted to, I guess, if we'd never found anything else. But . . ." He shrugged and shook his head.

Kelly turned to try to see Nick's face. "So there's nothing left there?"

"Nah. It's kind of a relief. Life changes what love means, you know? What I felt about Ty, it was a different kind of love."

"Have you found something else?" Kelly asked carefully, surprised by how nervous the question made him.

Nick looked at him oddly. "I don't know. Why are you asking me these things? This isn't some sort of post-gunshot meltdown, is it, 'cause I'm not built to handle those."

Kelly began to snicker, holding his chest so it wouldn't hurt. "I don't know. Maybe."

"If it is, we'll call Owen; he's good at the meltdown stuff."

"I'm not having a meltdown," Kelly assured him. "Are you seeing anyone?"

Nick was silent, sitting there and looking confused for a few seconds before answering. "Sort of. We haven't had a date or anything, but we're . . . actually, I'm not sure what we are."

The indecisive answer bolstered Kelly's courage and relieved him, which was an odd sensation. "Hey, Irish?"

Nick turned to him, the beginnings of a smile on his face.

"Will you kiss me?"

The smile faded into wide-eyed shock. Nick's eyes were so green he almost looked like a cartoon. Kelly began to laugh. He had to hold his hand over his wound, but he couldn't stop laughing. He reached out to put his other hand on Nick's arm. "I'm sorry I'm laughing," he wheezed. "It's the drugs, I swear."

Nick snorted and gently peeled Kelly's fingers off his forearm. "From now on you only get halves," he mumbled. He slid off the bed, beginning to chuckle.

"Wait!"

Nick turned, trying to look annoyed but still laughing. Kelly schooled his features, frowning dramatically. "I'm serious," he managed to say.

"Yeah, you look it," Nick drawled.

"I want you to kiss me."

Nick examined him, seeming dubious.

"I want to know what it feels like to kiss a guy. And you've had a lot of practice, so I know you're a good kisser."

"Are you simultaneously complimenting me and calling me a whore?"

"I'm . . . I'm just impressed you can take half a Percocet and say simul . . . simultaneous."

Nick sighed heavily, fighting back his smile. He came around the end of the bed and sat next to Kelly's hip, turning to hover over him. "Okay."

Kelly was surprised when his stomach flipped, but he liked the feeling. "Okay what?"

"Okay. If you want me to kiss you, I will."

"Really?"

Nick nodded. "But only if you can sit up on your own, and then pass a field sobriety test."

Kelly rolled his eyes and snorted. "You're such a dick."

"I'll give you that too if you want it," Nick said, laughing as he pushed off the bed and headed for the loft steps.

Kelly watched him, trying to decide if the flip in his stomach was excitement or nerves. "Hey!"

Nick stopped at the head of the staircase and turned again, ever patient.

"I'm serious," Kelly said.

Nick's eyes narrowed, and he remained there for a few moments before he moved slowly back to the bed. "You really want me to kiss you?"

"Yes."

"So you'll know what it feels like to kiss a guy."

"Yes."

"Why?"

"Well you and Ty both seem to enjoy it. What's good for you is good for me, right?"

"That's a horrible reason."

"Really?"

Nick sat down again, close enough that the mattress dipped and Kelly slid toward him. They stared at each other for a few seconds, Kelly holding his breath as Nick thought it through. He was curious, because he knew locking lips with another dude had to be different from kissing a woman, and he was by nature an inquisitive person. He was open to trying just about anything once, and he'd always kind of been on the fence about it. But he was also wondering what it would be like to kiss *Nick*, and that had nothing to do with the painkillers or his innate desire to try new things.

"Okay," Nick said quietly. He adjusted the way he was sitting, propping one hand on Kelly's other side as he leaned over him.

Kelly held up a finger. "No half-assed middle school kissing, either."

"Okay."

"I want the whole deal."

"This is starting to feel like I'm leasing a car or something."

"I'm serious, I want the Irish special."

Nick rolled his eyes and glanced up at the ceiling. "Fine. Jesus."

Kelly nodded, his lips twitching on a smile and his chest fluttering. They stared at each other as Nick leaned over him, and it was harder for Kelly to catch his breath as he waited for Nick to make his move. He licked his lips.

Nick finally laughed. "Close your eyes."

"Why?"

"'Cause I can't do this with you looking at me."

Kelly gave a long-suffering sigh, but he closed his eyes anyway, still fighting a smile. He felt Nick lean closer, and he inhaled sharply, holding his breath as Nick's lips brushed the corner of his mouth.

He parted his lips and tilted his head, their noses bumping as Nick moved the same way. They both laughed and Kelly cocked his head the other way, dragging his lower lip across Nick's as they adjusted. Then Nick was kissing him. *Really* kissing him. His lips parted, tongue darting between them to lick at Kelly's lips. His teeth closed over Kelly's lower lip and dragged before his tongue slipped inside Kelly's mouth.

They both moaned.

Kelly reached up and grabbed a handful of Nick's shirt, barely realizing he'd done it. His knuckles knocked against hard muscles. Nick's hand came up to Kelly's face, brushing his cheek tentatively as if he wasn't sure he was allowed to touch. Kelly nipped at his lip, and Nick groaned again. He pushed his hand under Kelly's head and clutched at his hair.

The stubble on Nick's chin scratched against Kelly's cheek. Nick leaned more on top of him, his hands clamping down in the kind of grip Kelly had never felt from a lover. The kiss was more forceful and demanding than any he'd ever experienced, and he found himself using his tongue and his teeth to fight back, even as he pulled Nick closer to urge him on.

Kelly's hand pressed against Nick's chest, and it wasn't even odd that there was nothing but muscle to grab there. He moaned again, and the sound traveled through his body, awakening the rest of him to the moment, to the scent of guns instead of roses, the brush of leather instead of lace.

Kelly gasped as Nick began to pull away. He didn't have the strength yet to sit up to follow. Their lips dragged as they separated. Nick's fingers released Kelly's hair and slid out from under him as he pushed himself up. Kelly finally opened his eyes, but he didn't let go of Nick's shirt. His heart was hammering and his mind was churning, making him light-headed.

"Well," Kelly finally breathed. "No shit."

Nick laughed and ran his thumb across his lip. Kelly knew him well enough to know when Nick was nervous, and he was nervous now. He tightened his grip on Nick's shirt to keep him from getting up. Nick turned hesitant green eyes on him, waiting for his verdict. Kelly had never really appreciated the color of Nick's eyes.

"Do that again," he whispered.

Nick took in a deep breath and then let it out slowly, like he was trying to calm himself. He patted Kelly's hand, taking it in his and gently extricating his shirt. "Let's just let that one settle with the Percocet, okay?"

He made to stand, and Kelly was forced to let him go.

"Yeah, okay."

Nick was walking away, running a hand through his hair, and Kelly realized his entire body was still buzzing. It might have been from the painkillers, but he was willing to place bets on his buddy right now.

It was the same feeling he got when his phone rang. The same feeling as waking up in the hospital to find Nick holding his hand. The same warmth of a blanket wrapping around his shoulders, and something inside him screamed for him to pursue it.

"Hey, Nick," he whispered.

Nick stopped and rolled his neck, like he might have been irritated by Kelly's repeated attempts to keep him from descending the stairs. He turned, though, the same easy smile on his face, his feelings masked by his legendary patience.

"Is the rest of it like that too?" Kelly asked.

Nick ran his teeth across his lip, beginning to nod. "Isn't it always if you have the right dance partner?"

Kelly stared at him, finding himself nodding. Jesus, was it possible he was considering Nick O'Flaherty a dance partner right now? Yes. Yes, he was.

"You're not going to ask me to fuck you now, are you?" Nick asked, deadpan.

Kelly began to laugh. "The thought was crossing my mind."

Nick's smile faded. "Are you serious?"

"Sort of. You got the engine revved a little."

Nick rolled his eyes and turned toward the stairs. "Put him back in the garage then. I don't drive automatics," he said as he thumped down the stairs.

Nick woke with a jerk as a hand grabbed at his arm. He peered over in the moonlight. "You okay?"

"I need to move," Kelly grunted.

They'd shared enough beds—and floors—over the years that Nick knew Kelly slept on his side. Being forced to sleep flat on his back made him restless and miserable, but he hadn't recovered the strength in his torso yet to roll onto his side without help or something to grab onto and pull.

Nick fumbled for the pillows he'd stacked between them and tossed them to the foot of the bed, rolling onto his side and holding his arm out. "Come on."

Kelly used Nick's forearm to pull himself to his side, and as soon as he was settled, Nick took the spare pillows and wedged them behind Kelly's back to rest against. He was hyperaware of how close he was, of his breaths hitting Kelly's cheek as he reached across him. Goddammit, why had he even agreed to that kiss in the first place? Now the next day or so would be awkward as hell as he tried to forget how fucking good Kelly felt in his arms.

Once he was certain there was support behind Kelly, he took the pillow he'd been using and pushed it against Kelly's chest to give him something to hold.

"I don't need that," Kelly mumbled. He shoved the pillow back toward the head of the bed.

Nick scowled. "You always hold something when you sleep."

"I'm not taking your pillow. Quit it."

Nick huffed and laid back down, facing Kelly. He watched him for several minutes, alert for signs of pain or misery, waiting for his breathing to even out. It didn't though, and finally Kelly opened his eyes again.

"You hurting?" Nick asked him.

"A little. Not enough to take anything. I just can't sleep."

Nick remained silent, waiting for Kelly to go on. If he needed to get something off his chest, he would. And Nick had a feeling he knew exactly what Kelly needed to discuss.

"It was a good kiss," Kelly finally said.

Nick huffed a laugh. "Yes, it was."

"What does that mean?"

"It means I'm a fabulous kisser and you're easy."

Kelly rolled his eyes.

Nick watched and waited, but finally he got tired of the weighty silence. "Are you asking me if it means you're gay if you liked one kiss?"

"Maybe."

"Well, I don't have any answers. I'm leaning toward no."

Kelly sighed loudly. "I still want you to do it again. Does that matter?"

Nick's chest fluttered. He had to fight for enough breath to answer. "You mean does it matter in the grand scheme of things?"

"I mean does it matter to you?"

Nick caught his breath, afraid to break the silence as they stared across the dim inches. He had spent years trying to avoid thinking of his closest friends in a sexual way. It had been especially difficult with Kelly at first, because they were both touchy-feely people. Eventually, years of camaraderie had whitewashed the physical nature of their friendship, but that one fucking kiss had taken down those mental barriers in a heartbeat. Did it matter to him that Kelly might be struggling with his sexual identity after all these years? Yes. Did it matter to him that Kelly had chosen him to try to help him answer those questions? Yes.

Did it matter to him that he wanted nothing more than to grab Kelly's face and kiss him again until neither of them could breathe, that he wanted to feel Kelly's body against his now, that his mind had gone into overdrive and couldn't seem to stop spinning the moment Kelly's fingers had grasped at his T-shirt? Did it matter that Kelly was saying he wanted the same thing? "It does matter to me."

"Will you give me more?" Kelly whispered.

Nick let out his pent-up breath and closed his eyes, shaking his head. Something akin to terror streaked through him, followed swiftly by lust. Giving Kelly more would mean ramifications neither of them could deal with. It would mean altering the state of their friendship, *risking* it, and for what?

"I'm not under the influence anymore. Much. Even if I was, I've done things way worse than you that I've never regretted."

Nick barked a laugh, and they both began to chuckle. Suddenly the tension was gone again and it was just the Devil Doc in bed with him once more. Kelly reached across the space between them and brushed his fingers over Nick's knuckles. A scar on the back of Nick's hand still displayed the tiny railroad tracks where Kelly had stitched a gash in the field. He ran his fingers across it. There were half a dozen other places on Nick's body that he'd stitched up over the years. Nick knew his hands well. He'd never seen them as anything but healing hands, though, not until the moment Kelly's fingers had clutched at his shirt and pulled him closer as they'd kissed.

"Do you want to?" Kelly asked.

"Yes, but . . ." Nick splayed his fingers, and Kelly's twined with them, grasping his hand. Kelly gave his fingers a tug and Nick slid across the inches between them. Their lips met, and once again it stole Nick's breath from his lungs, sped his heart until his ears buzzed, flushed his body with ice and fire. Kelly pulled his hand loose and grabbed Nick's elbow, pulling at it until he was able to get his hand under the sleeve and against Nick's skin.

"How's this work?" Kelly gasped. His lips moved against Nick's, and Nick groaned.

"It doesn't work at all. You can't even roll over by yourself."

He reached around Kelly and pushed at the pillows he'd been so careful to arrange, then he wrapped his arm around him and dragged him close enough to press against him. They'd shared a bed hundreds of times, and more often than not they'd woken up cuddling. Kelly somehow always managed to end up the big spoon. Maybe they could keep this within the realm of something they understood. Maybe.

"You saying you can't handle that?" Kelly needled, grinning.

Nick could see that grin in the moonlight, had seen that grin a thousand times before. Now, though, he wanted to wipe it away with another kiss. Jesus, if they didn't do something about this now, it was going to linger.

He pushed Kelly flat, then reached across him and flipped the lamp on so he could see Kelly's face more clearly. Kelly groaned as his erection rubbed against Nick's thigh. The teasing smile disappeared.

"God, that feels weird," Kelly huffed.

"Say the word and I'll stop," Nick grunted, although he was silently praying Kelly would do no such thing. He would never be able to look at Kelly's hands the same way again, but at least this way they might get it out of their systems.

Kelly shifted his shoulders, staring at Nick with wide eyes. Nick had him pinned to the mattress. One of Kelly's hands had found its way all the way under Nick's shirt to drag down the giant eagle, globe, and anchor tattoo on Nick's shoulder, and he'd thrown one foot over Nick's calf as their legs tangled together. They were both hard.

"It feels good," Kelly finally whispered, sounding surprised. "Will it hurt?"

"I'm not going to fuck you, Kels."

"Why not?"

"Because you're hurt and I get rough."

Kelly swallowed hard, his breath quickening. "How rough?"

Nick cocked his head and smiled slowly.

"That's kind of hot."

Nick stretched out over him and kissed him, careful not to rest his full weight on him, eliciting a louder groan from Kelly. He shifted until he could feel Kelly's erection against his through his boxers.

"Jesus, Nick," Kelly gasped, finally dropping the humor in his voice. He pushed at Nick's shirt. "Lose some of this."

Nick shoved up and tugged at his shirt with his free hand, yanking it over his head and throwing it aside. Kelly ran his hand up Nick's chest, fingers barely grazing, tentative. He was an odd mixture of bold and uncertain. Nick didn't know why that turned him on, but it did. He'd never been with anyone for their first time. He'd certainly never been with a friend. Oh God, this was probably a bad idea. But something about it felt like a *great* idea as Kelly met his eyes, and Nick couldn't deny him anything in that moment.

"Go ahead," Nick grunted.

Kelly laughed again, his body relaxing even more. He dragged his fingers along the muscles of Nick's abdomen, never taking his eyes off Nick's. Nick fought to regulate his breathing, but it was getting difficult. He gasped when Kelly's hand dipped under the elastic of his boxers, and he lowered himself to nip at Kelly's lips.

"Seriously, how rough are you?" Kelly asked, his voice husky.

"When you get healed up, maybe I'll show you."

Kelly's breaths came harder and faster. "Can you show me a little?"

Nick laughed, kissing Kelly one more time before he got to his hands and knees. Kelly shoved at his boxers, pushing them down to his thighs. With the material out of the way, his fingers dragged back across Nick's hips and up his ribs.

Nick hovered over him, meeting his eyes and trying to read just how serious he was. Kelly was the same person who'd insisted it would be fun to BASE jump the Grand Canyon and had begged Nick to go with him to Nicaragua to go volcano boarding. He never thought things through to their natural end. That was Nick's job. "Reaching the point of no return on this."

"I've been awake for an hour, Nick. Couldn't stop thinking about it."

Nick's breath caught. Kelly'd been lying awake thinking about this. Thinking about him. Any reservations that had remained went out the window with that. Nick shoved away from him so he could tug his sleep bottoms down for him. He didn't even try to get the pants all the way off, just pulled them to Kelly's knees before bending his head to place a kiss at Kelly's hip.

Kelly's entire body jerked and he gasped, reaching down to grab a handful of Nick's hair. Nick glanced up and grinned as he met Kelly's eyes. Kelly was watching him, biting his tongue. Nick ducked his head to lick at him, but Kelly's hand in his hair stopped him. His nerves tumbled, and Nick looked up again, expecting to see indecision on Kelly's face. Instead, Kelly was smiling.

"Better make it good," Kelly drawled. "No pressure."

Nick grunted at him. Yeah. He did need to make it good. In case this was the only chance Kelly gave him. And in case it wasn't . . .

"And no biting!"

"You have more rules than the Marine Corps," Nick mumbled. "Shut up."

To make his point, he dragged his teeth across Kelly's hip bone and bit down. Kelly was still squirming and cussing at him when Nick took his cock into his mouth and all the way to the back of his throat in one swift motion.

"Holy Jesus!" Kelly cried, and his other hand landed on Nick's shoulder. The sound of the slap echoed off the loft's sloped ceiling. Nick raised his head slowly, letting Kelly's cock slide between his lips, curling his tongue around the head before he licked at the tip one last time and looked up at Kelly again.

Kelly wasn't smiling anymore. "You can bite," he gasped as he began to kick out of his pajama bottoms. "You can do whatever the fuck you want to."

"Good to know," Nick purred, smirking. "What I want to do isn't really on the table yet."

Kelly's chest heaved with the deep breaths he was taking. Nick slid a hand under his thigh and raised his leg, remembering to be careful as he hefted it onto his shoulder. He bent his head and licked at the crease of Kelly's thigh. They shared a grin, and Kelly began to chuckle.

"I remember sharing a wall with you, O'Flaherty. I know how dirty you are."

Nick nodded and licked at the head of his cock, sucking it into his mouth. He sucked until Kelly's hand tightened in his hair again, then he forced Kelly's cock to the back of his throat and swallowed around it. Kelly shouted, starting to cuss and call Nick names he usually only heard when they were playing paintball.

He sucked Kelly up and down one last time and then pushed at his leg, rolling Kelly's hips back. He licked at his balls and then moved his lips over them, massaging them, humming as he did it. Kelly's leg began to tighten over his shoulder, and Nick took the cue and sucked one of his balls into his mouth.

"Son of a bitch! Fuck! How are you doing that?"

Nick hummed in response, and Kelly began to writhe. He twisted, his heel digging into Nick's spine, his hand pulling Nick's hair hard enough that Nick raised his head. He grabbed Kelly's wrist and jerked it away from his hair, pinning it to the mattress beside Kelly's hip.

"Tell me to stop if you need to," he growled. "But don't pull my fucking hair out."

Kelly nodded fervently.

Nick began to stroke his cock, using the hand he had wrapped around Kelly's thigh. He sucked on his finger as Kelly watched him from under lowered lashes.

"This gonna hurt?" Kelly asked.

"I won't hurt you," Nick whispered. He pressed his wet finger against the muscles around Kelly's asshole, not hard enough to enter him, just to let him feel something there.

Kelly's heel dug into his back. His fingers clutched at the sheet beside him. "God, that feels weird!"

Nick shook his head and dragged his palm over Kelly's thigh. "You are way too tense for that," he muttered.

He let Kelly's leg slide down his arm, then he crawled up Kelly's body, sliding his cock against Kelly's leg, careful not to settle his weight on Kelly's abdomen.

"I'm not tense," Kelly argued as soon as Nick was looking him in the eyes again. "I'm just trying not to fucking come all over you two seconds after you touched me. How the hell did you do the swallowing thing?"

Nick laughed, lowering himself, careful to avoid Kelly's wound as he stretched out against his body. Kelly was shorter than him by a few inches and more compact, but he was all hard muscle and dry wit.

"You realize coming all over me is sort of what I'm going for, right?"

Kelly breathed out hard. His hand came to rest against Nick's ribs, then dragged lower, shoving between their bodies. Nick had to push up to let him reach between them, and then Kelly's fingers were wrapping around his cock. Nick's breath stuttered and his eyes fell shut. He lowered his head to press his forehead against Kelly's. Their noses smashed together. Kelly lifted his chin for a kiss, then began to stroke Nick, his lips mimicking the lazy rhythm. Nick groaned.

"You're so fucking hot, you know that?" Kelly whispered.

"I bet you tell that to all your oldest friends as you're jacking them off."

Kelly snickered and arched his back, seeking contact. "No, just you."

Nick propped himself on one elbow and sought Kelly's cock with his other hand. Their knuckles brushed as they gripped each other. Nick thrust his hips into Kelly's.

Kelly bit at Nick's lip, smiling. "You remember that trip to San Diego when we shared a hotel room and you hooked up with that freaky blonde?"

Nick grunted, nodding. "Odd time to bring it up."

"I watched you," Kelly admitted, closing his eyes. "Whenever I need to get off, I think about that night. I always thought it was the girl, but now I'm thinking maybe . . ."

"You're thinking way too much," Nick snarled. He didn't want to hear that, no matter how much the implications made his stomach flutter or his heart race. He grabbed Kelly's hands and slammed both into the mattress, holding him by his wrists. He thrust his hips, sliding his leaking cock along Kelly's. "What you should be thinking about is wrapping your legs around me," he said against Kelly's lips before kissing him. He licked at Kelly's teeth and then sucked on his tongue.

Kelly groaned and absently tried to pull both knees up. He cursed in frustration when he couldn't manage it, and Nick fumbled at his side to help him. Kelly nodded almost frantically, and Nick helped him to move and slide his feet over Nick's thighs.

Nick continued to rut against him, pressing down hard, cocks sliding, balls pressing together. It would be so easy in this position to just put the head of his cock against Kelly's ass and shove himself in. That was good to know for next time.

"Now you should be thinking about me fucking you," he hissed. "Because I sure as hell am."

"Oh God," Kelly breathed.

"No, you don't say his name when I fuck you. You say mine."

Kelly responded with an inarticulate gasp.

Nick shoved his hips hard against Kelly's, their cocks both leaking, gliding against sweaty muscles. He put his lips against Kelly's ear. "Are you thinking about me inside you?"

Kelly grunted and shuddered. "Fuck yes."

"That's all you should be thinking, you understand?"

Kelly nodded jerkily. Nick released one of his hands and dragged his palm up Kelly's neck and chin, shoving one finger into his mouth. Kelly moaned and sucked it in, wrapping his tongue around it and covering Nick's finger in saliva. He seemed to instinctively know what Nick intended to do, and he obliged.

Nick reached between them and used his slick finger to push at those stubborn muscles again, this time forcing the blunt tip past them.

"Nick!" Kelly gasped.

"That's right. What's the only thing you're thinking?" Nick growled.

"You inside me," Kelly recited breathlessly. "Your big fucking dick in there."

Nick used the tip of his finger to press at those muscles but didn't go deeper, fighting his orgasm. The idea of being inside Kelly when either of them came was almost too much.

Kelly clutched at him, squirming under him, writhing against his cock, pushing at Nick's finger and forcing the muscles to fight back. "Fuck, Nick!"

"Come for me," Nick whispered. "Scream my fucking name."

He bent and kissed him, a brutal clash of tongues and teeth as Kelly bucked under him, crying out against his lips. It wasn't Nick's name, but it was close enough. The first jolt of his orgasm hit and he pulled his finger away, holding Kelly down by both arms as he rutted against him, adding hot spurts of cum to the sweat already mingling between them.

He pushed up to his knees to take his cock in hand and stroke himself through the rest of the orgasm. They both watched greedily as he came all over Kelly's lower abs.

Kelly's cock was pulsing, cum dripping down its side. He reached to finish himself off, but Nick batted his hand away and scooted down until he could lick that cum off and suck the head into his mouth. Kelly's hand landed in his hair again, and he shoved up into Nick's mouth as he shot the rest of his load down Nick's throat.

When Kelly's fingers finally loosened their grip, Nick collapsed beside him in the bed, gasping in time with Kelly's gulps for air.

"Jesus fucking Christ, O'Flaherty," Kelly finally stuttered.

"You hurt?"

"My fucking . . . mind. My mind is blown."

Nick laughed weakly and sat up. "You want water?"

Kelly grabbed his arm, stopping him and pulling him off balance so he toppled back to his side. He gazed up into Kelly's eyes in the harsh lamplight. Nick had always loved Kelly's oddly colored eyes, but he'd never imagined he'd be looking into them like this.

"'You don't say his name, you say mine'?" Kelly repeated incredulously. "I almost came right then, where the fuck have you been hiding that?"

Nick grinned and rested on his elbow. "Oh God, Kels, what have we done here?"

"I don't care. We're exploring this further." Kelly waved a finger in Nick's face.

"Okay," Nick agreed. He reached across Kelly's body, bending to kiss him as he grabbed the bottle of painkillers off the bedside table.

They continued the kiss as Nick popped the lid off the bottle, and Kelly moaned plaintively when Nick pulled away.

"Fucker," Kelly muttered.

Nick broke one of the pills in half and offered one half to Kelly with a cheeky grin. "In place of a cigarette?"

Kelly took the pill, watching with narrowed eyes as Nick popped the other half in his mouth. They shared a bottle of water, laughing as they used one of the spare pillows to clean off.

As they were settling down to sleep, Nick began to build the pillow barrier between them again. Kelly reached out and stopped him.

"I think if I can handle what we just did, I can take it if you accidentally roll over in the middle of the night."

Nick raised an eyebrow. "You sure?"

Kelly nodded and grinned. "Are you too butch to cuddle?"

Nick rolled his eyes and laid himself out, scooting closer to Kelly and resting his head in the crook of his arm. "We'll discuss this tomorrow," he muttered, closing his eyes and letting the exhaustion take over.

Kelly laughed, running his fingers through Nick's hair. "Oh yeah, we will."

Kelly woke when the warmth of the sun touched his face. He turned away from it, reaching out across the bed. His hand hit empty space, though, and he finally opened his eyes and raised his head.

"Irish?" he said, voice hoarse from sleep.

Nick was gone, though, and his side of the bed was cold under Kelly's fingers. Kelly struggled to sit, using the covers and the mattress to pull himself up.

"Loved me and left me. Typical O'Flaherty," Kelly muttered. He probably should have been a nervous wreck waking up alone after last night, especially since Nick was a proven flight risk when it came to relationships. But then he glanced at the clock on the table out of habit and saw a note there instructing him to call for help if he needed it. He smiled at Nick's blunt, no-frills handwriting. His pills were lined up for him, and a glass of water sat within arm's reach.

He managed to drag himself out of bed and make it to the bathroom without too much trouble. Wiping his stomach clean with a damp rag and brushing his teeth was all the effort he put into his appearance, though.

He was wiping some other guy's spunk off his stomach. Jesus. It wasn't just some other guy, either. It was *Nick*. It was his best friend. It was his best friend he'd always thought was straight until a year ago. What did that even fucking mean for him? Could Kelly still call himself straight? Was he gay now? God, he hoped Nick had some answers for him because Nick was the only person he could think of to even ask these things.

He turned to examine himself in the mirror. "Really?" he whispered to his reflection. He nodded and began to grin without meaning to. "Okay then. You stupid asshole."

He pulled on a pair of sweat pants and a ragged T-shirt, but he had to sit on the end of the bed and rest after he was dressed. He was hard-pressed not to laugh at himself. Too weak to dress himself without a breather, but not too fucking weak to beg his best friend to fuck him.

He caught sight of the pajama bottoms he'd been wearing last night, crumpled at the foot of the bed where he'd kicked them. His stomach fluttered, and again he was surprised by the reaction. Nick had been good. Very good. Jizz-in-your-pants good. Everything about it had been good, and Kelly was shockingly okay with that. What made him kind of want to throw up was wondering how Nick was taking it.

He winced as he stood, fighting past the pull as he shuffled toward the stairs. The painkillers hadn't kicked in yet, and mornings were always the worst. He stood at the top of the steps, looking down. It seemed like a long way without someone there to catch him if he fell.

Nick appeared at the bottom of the staircase, peering up at him. "You need help?"

"I thought I didn't," Kelly said with a grin. "I might have been wrong."

Nick took the stairs two at a time, coming to the step below him and letting him lean on his shoulders. Nick's arm slipped around his waist, and Kelly's entire body shivered. Nick's scent, the way he gripped Kelly's shirt, the warmth of his body, all brought back memories of last night with a confusing rush of sensations.

"You too stubborn to call for help now?" Nick muttered.

"I guess."

Nick glanced up at him, frowning. Kelly was silent as they fumbled their way down the stairs. He couldn't quite catch his breath, and he wasn't used to the way his chest kept filling with butterflies.

When he'd asked Nick to kiss him last night, he'd never anticipated this lingering result.

He didn't get a chance to study Nick's face again until he was easing into his recliner. He looked up as Nick bent over him. Nick didn't seem flustered. He didn't seem nervous or scared or confused or any of the other myriad of emotions Kelly had felt in the last two minutes. But then, when had Nick ever looked nervous?

"Doc?" Nick said pointedly.

"Huh?"

"I asked you if you wanted food," Nick said with a smile. "Are you okay?"

Kelly nodded, closing his eyes and grimacing as he tried to get comfortable. He jumped when Nick patted his cheek.

"You hurting?" Nick asked.

"Is it that obvious?"

Nick nodded, his frown deepening. "Did I hurt you?" he asked, voice going softer.

Kelly grinned slowly. That intimate tone of voice, talking about what they'd done last night, was something he found surprisingly sexy.

"Kels?"

Kelly ran a gentle finger over his bullet wound and shrugged. "It bled a little. Maybe a stitch pulled loose or something."

Nick's gaze dropped to Kelly's wound, and his face paled. "Shit."

Kelly reached out and ran a hand over Nick's palm, making sure Nick was looking into his eyes again before he spoke. "I wasn't feeling anything last night but good."

Nick looked both relieved and amused.

"What are you fixing?" Kelly asked to get Nick's mind off how delicate Kelly still was. Nick was an exceptional cook. They'd discovered that when they'd been stationed at Lejeune and had all gone in to rent a house together. Nick's job had always been to cook.

"What do you want?"

Kelly shrugged, shaking his head. He wasn't really in the mood for food.

Nick sighed and sat on the edge of the coffee table, his hands clasped between his knees. "This is last night catching up to you, isn't it?" he asked, voice grim.

Kelly's breath caught. He made the mistake of meeting Nick's eyes, and he was caught by them, transfixed by their color, by the earnest concern in them.

Nick inhaled deeply. "There's nothing I can say right now that won't be awkward."

Kelly began to laugh. "I know it. We don't have to talk about it."

"I kind of think we do," Nick said. "Eventually we'll have to. I don't know about you, but I don't like the feeling of having something hanging between us."

"Neither do I," Kelly whispered.

"And right now there's a wicked big thing hanging there."

Kelly snorted.

"I'm sorry."

"What for?" Kelly blurted.

Nick shrugged, looking around the room with a little smile. "I feel like I took advantage of you being drugged."

"But you didn't."

"But I feel like I did," Nick insisted.

"Yeah but, if you hadn't, you'd be feeling guilty for telling me no," Kelly argued.

"No I wouldn't," Nick said. A smile pulled at his lips. "I'd be *regretting* telling you no and probably very frustrated, but . . ."

The admission warmed Kelly all the way to his toes. "So that's how you do it," he muttered.

"What?"

"I just learned the secret to the O'Flaherty charm," Kelly said, beginning to grin. "You just . . . stun the other person with honesty."

Nick chuckled, his cheeks beginning to flush. But he didn't look away. They stared at each other, getting lost in the familiarity for long seconds before Nick leaned closer. "Are you okay, Kels? And I don't mean the hole in your chest."

Kelly nodded. Then he frowned. "No, actually."

Nick's face clouded over, his brow furrowing and his eyes apprehensive.

"See, every time I think about you now, I get these butterflies," Kelly explained, fluttering his fingers at his chest. "And it's weird because it's you, and you're you. But I like it too. And . . . I like that it's you. So I'm not sure what to do with that."

Nick licked his lips, leaving his tongue at the corner of his mouth like he always did when he was thinking. Kelly's eyes were drawn to it briefly before he tore his attention away and focused back on Nick's eyes.

"I don't know what to tell you," Nick finally said.

"How about telling me it'll pass? Or that it's just the drugs. Or almost dying. Come on, O'Flaherty, I know you have half a dozen excuses at the ready to use for things like this."

Nick was silent, chewing on his lip.

Kelly's smile fell. "Don't you?"

"I've never run into a thing like this," Nick admitted.

Kelly cocked his head. "You feel it too, don't you?"

Nick laughed. "Butterflies whenever I think about myself?"

"Don't play word games with me, smart-ass. The meds haven't kicked in yet."

Nick sighed and contemplated his hands. He dragged his thumb over the scar on the back of his hand. "I think it's unproductive to talk about it until you've recovered a little more." He looked up, forcing a smile to cover the hint of fear Kelly could see in his eyes.

Kelly wanted to push, to get past that smile and see just what Nick was thinking, what he was afraid of. Because the prospects last night had opened up were all parading past Kelly's mind, and he liked what he saw. He needed Nick to be on the same page with him, though, and Nick obviously wasn't yet. Kelly knew one thing for certain, and that was that Nick wouldn't be pushed, he wouldn't be bullied, and he sure as hell wouldn't turn that page faster if Kelly tried to do it for him.

So Kelly just nodded. "How about pancakes?"

"With M&M's?"

"You have some?" Kelly asked, his eyes going wider and his mouth beginning to water.

Nick gave him a sly grin and stood. He patted Kelly's head as he walked by him, heading for the kitchen.

"Wait a minute," Kelly grunted, reaching out to grasp Nick's arm. "That's all I get the morning after?"

Nick stutter-stepped and backtracked to look down at Kelly. "What? I gave you drugs and I'm fixing your breakfast on a tray, what more do you want?"

Kelly grinned and gave Nick's arm a little tug. He could see Nick biting his tongue when he smiled, and something about it kicked Kelly's sex drive into gear. "You're really going to make me ask for it?"

Nick raised an eyebrow, smiling wider.

Kelly rolled his eyes and sagged his shoulders, tugging Nick again. "Give me a kiss!"

Nick sighed, glancing around the room as he fought a smile. He might have been trying to come up with a reason not to, or he might have been fighting the fact that he wanted to. He finally put a hand on Kelly's head and bent over him, narrowing his eyes when he peered into Kelly's. He smiled and pressed his nose and lips against Kelly's cheek before giving him a gentle kiss, then moved away before Kelly could seek more, leaving Kelly sitting there filled with warmth and nerves.

Kelly smiled, watching Nick's reflection in the dark television as he moved around in the kitchen, making Kelly's pancakes. Nick knew he liked pancakes with M&M's in them. Kelly had *married* a woman who'd never even known such a simple fact about him, who'd never cared to learn.

He let himself ponder that. Ponder Nick. Every time he'd woken up in the hospital in New Orleans, Nick had been there. Sometimes Ty had been there as well, sitting with him, talking with Nick, or curled up asleep in the chair in the corner. But Nick had been there every time without fail. He'd sat in the chair and read. He'd slept curled up on the couch that was too short for him, or with his head resting on the bed near Kelly's hand. He'd stolen Kelly's lunch instead of leaving to go to the cafeteria, and then called to get him more when he woke.

Nick hadn't left his side, and when the time had come for Kelly to be discharged, Nick hadn't even discussed coming home with him. He'd simply assumed he would. People searched their entire lives for someone to just care about them. Somehow Kelly had taken that feeling for granted.

Nick returned and set a plate of pancakes down on the table by Kelly's side. Kelly watched him, still caught up on the idea of someone who would literally lay down his life for him, who had almost done so on several occasions. Kelly had loved Nick for years, just like he loved the rest of the team. Who was to say that couldn't be more? Where was it written that either of them had to go through life looking for someone who understood them when they had each other right here? Why did that have to be off the table just because Kelly had spent his entire life pursuing women? He felt like a door had been opened last night, a door he'd never known existed.

Nick had a toothpick in his mouth, chewing on it as he laid out Kelly's breakfast where he could reach it. Kelly plucked the toothpick out. "Dangerous," he grumbled.

Nick snorted, but as he was turning away, Kelly grabbed his shirtfront and pulled him closer. Nick almost stumbled over the side table, and he had to put both hands on the arms of Kelly's chair to keep himself from pitching forward into Kelly's lap. His eyes were wide.

"How long do I have to recover, exactly?" Kelly demanded.

"What?"

"How long are you going to fumble around before you'll sit back down and talk to me?"

Nick blinked a few times, his eyes seeming to turn greener as Kelly watched. Kelly smiled, growing warmer. He tightened his grip on Nick's shirtfront so the man couldn't escape.

"Look, I love you," Kelly told him. "You love me. We've bled for each other. Why can't that turn into more?"

"Kels . . ."

"Stop. Before you argue with me, just think about it objectively without adding in who we are."

"Who we are is kind of a big deal."

Kelly let him go and took a deep breath. "Sit down, I want to talk about this."

Nick didn't sit. Instead he leaned closer, close enough that Kelly's heart stuttered and he closed his eyes. He could feel Nick's breath on his lips, feel the scratch of stubble against his chin. "Your pancakes are getting cold," Nick whispered before pulling back.

Kelly's eyes drifted open to stare at the plate of perfect golden pancakes with melting M&M's made into smiley face patterns. He laughed and met Nick's eyes again. Nick was grinning. He hesitated briefly before he pressed another gentle kiss to Kelly's lips. This time he extended it, turning it a little less chaste and adding a little more tongue and teeth.

Kelly took stock of his racing heart, his shallow breaths, the fluttering in his stomach. He hadn't felt like this since he'd been a teenager, and he liked it. It wasn't some stranger in a smoky bar giving him that adventurous feeling, either, it was one of his oldest and dearest friends. He tried to push forward to deepen the kiss, but Nick pulled away from him, running his thumb over his lips.

"Eat. I'm not fixing you more," Nick muttered. He stepped away, but his hand landed on Kelly's shoulder and squeezed. "We'll talk after. I promise."

Kelly nodded, satisfied. Because Nick O'Flaherty always kept his promises.

When Kelly woke, he realized Nick had just waited for his painkillers to kick in and then given him the slip. He had opened up the windows and the doors to the back deck to allow the breeze to sweep through the cabin, then gone outside and hadn't come back before Kelly began to doze.

Kelly struggled with the lever on the side of the recliner and finally got the leg down so he could try to stand. He gasped at the pain and stopped moving as soon as he stood, afraid to take another step. His painkillers had worn off. How long had he been asleep?

"Irish?" he called out.

He heard a thump from outside on the deck, and Nick's footfalls were heavy as he jogged to the door. He appeared in the doorway, the sunlight streaming in around him. He'd changed into jeans and a loose flannel shirt, and with the scruff and his curly hair getting longer, he looked pretty damn at home in Kelly's cabin in the middle of the woods. He also had his combat knife strapped to his thigh.

A frown creased Kelly's brow. "What are you doing?"

"What are *you* doing?" Nick asked as he made his way over. "Why didn't you call for help?"

"I just did."

Nick ducked under the arm Kelly raised, sliding his hand around Kelly's waist to help support him. "You want to go back down?"

"No. What are you doing outside? Can I go out there?"

"Yeah, but sit first," Nick muttered. Kelly didn't really have much choice as Nick lowered him back to the chair. "I'll go get your pills; let them settle before you move again."

Kelly sighed and waited, staring at the open door as the breeze kicked up. It smelled of sunshine and pine, with a hint of crisp air left from the winter. He loved spring and fall for weather like this. He looked forward to the sunlight on his face.

Nick thumped back down the steps with his pills and water bottle.

"What were you doing outside?" Kelly asked, looking pointedly at the knife on Nick's thigh.

Nick grinned lopsidedly and handed him his pills. "I'll show you."

Kelly downed the pills, then held his arm out for help. He slid it around Nick's neck, an action they'd repeated dozens of times over the last week or so. But this time felt different. This time Kelly's fingers dug into Nick's triceps, appreciating the strength in Nick's frame. This time Kelly's nose lingered at Nick's temple, taking in his scent and letting it stir everything from his mind to his body.

"Wow," Kelly murmured. "So that's still there."

Nick's breath gusted against his cheek. "Yeah, it is."

Kelly looked up into his eyes, hoping to catch a glimpse of what Nick was really feeling and thinking. He still appeared scared and worried, his brow furrowed and his eyes hesitant, but there was fire there too. He wanted to explore this as badly as Kelly did, but he was holding back for obvious reasons.

Kelly grinned. "Kiss me again."

"Kels—"

"You remember what you told me last night? The only thing I should be thinking about was . . ."

Nick inhaled sharply, his breath stuttering as he and Kelly stared at each other. "Me inside you."

Just the words made Kelly's breath catch. "Kiss me again, dammit."

Nick gave a curt nod, then he reached up to caress Kelly's cheek before he leaned closer and pressed their lips together. It was another careful kiss, a mere brush of lips with a hint of Nick's teeth on Kelly's lower lip before he leaned back. Kelly swayed forward, left breathless and light-headed by that simple, gentle touch.

Nick's hand pressed to the small of Kelly's back to pull their bodies together, holding him tight so he wouldn't fall. Kelly grabbed the back of his neck, delving into another kiss with a bit more fervor than their first. It was so natural for it to turn into a passionate embrace, Kelly had to wonder why they'd never done it before.

Kelly would have let it go on all day, but Nick had more self-control than he did. He gently pulled away, holding Kelly's face so Kelly couldn't chase him.

"Come on," he whispered finally. "I'll show you what I was doing outside."

Kelly grunted, but he allowed Nick to lead him out there. He was no longer interested in the outdoors or sunshine or whatever Nick had been up to, he just wanted Nick to kiss him again. He winced as the sun hit his eyes, but it felt good to be outside. He put his face up to the warmth and let out a sigh of relief.

"Feels good, right?" Nick murmured.

Kelly nodded, opening his eyes to regard Nick again.

"Can you stand? Walk?"

"Yeah, I'm good," Kelly said. He watched as Nick moved away, seeing his dear friend in a completely new light. The way Nick's shoulders moved, the way he walked with a slight limp he'd never be able to fully hide as he aged because of the shrapnel embedded in his femur, the way his left hand stayed near the handle of his knife. These were all things Kelly'd noticed before, but now he was equating them to the way the muscles of Nick's back felt under his fingers, the way Nick's hips rolled between his thighs, and the myriad of things Nick could do with his scarred hands.

Nick picked up a stick from the railing as Kelly moved gingerly toward the Adirondack chairs in the corner of the deck. Nick turned and held up the stick, grinning. He'd shaved the bark from it, smoothing the shaft, and he'd crafted the bulbous end into curved fingers, all with blunt tips. Kelly laughed as Nick handed it to him.

"A back scratcher?"

Nick shrugged, smiling. "I remember when I broke my collarbone, I was always itching and never able to get to it. You can also use it to reach things so you won't have to strain to get them."

Kelly ran his thumb over the tips of the fingers, nodding. "Thanks, Irish."

"You're welcome." Nick leaned against the railing, crossing his arms. "You want to try a walk?"

Kelly groaned, but he nodded. He was supposed to walk every day. "Might as well get it over with."

"I'll grab you some shoes."

He jogged back inside, leaving Kelly to ponder the homemade back scratcher. Nick wasn't the type of guy who needed to be moving or doing something. He didn't need to have something to do with his hands all the time. He could easily relax in a deck chair and lose himself in his thoughts for hours, or sit and read a book, or just chill under the stars. He hadn't been out here making this to keep himself busy while Kelly napped.

When Kelly looked up again, Nick was standing in the doorway watching him. "I can try again if it won't work."

"No, it's good."

"We'll find you a cane too," Nick added, smirking.

"Unless it has a sword in it, I don't want a cane."

Nick snickered, coming closer with Kelly's boots. He patted the top of his head as he knelt at Kelly's feet. "Hold on."

Kelly's breath caught. He rested his hand on Nick's head to keep his balance and peered down at Nick as he slid one foot into the boot Nick was holding for him. They got both boots on, and Nick was tying them up for him before Kelly realized he still had his hand in Nick's hair. He drew his fingers through the growing curls.

Nick glanced up at him as he pulled the first bow tight. He smiled knowingly when Kelly didn't loosen his hold on his hair, then ducked his head and tied the second boot. Kelly had always thought Nick a handsome man, in the same way he appreciated the beauty of a spring day or the sunrise on a misty morning. He'd never equated that appreciation with sex or desire, though, so the stirring in his groin when he remembered Nick's body against his, or when Nick knelt in front of him, was completely new.

He narrowed his eyes. When Nick stood, he mirrored Kelly's expression and leaned against the railing. They stared at one another as birds chirped and the wind rustled the leaves above them.

"I'm so confused right now," Kelly admitted.

"I know," Nick said, his voice soft and somehow comforting. "Me too."

"What do we do? Go for it? Pretend it didn't happen? Talk it out?"

"I remember my first time," Nick said, shaking his head. "You'll have to talk about it. You will. And I'm the only one here."

"So we talk it out."

Nick nodded.

"Have you ever wanted to fuck me before?" Kelly demanded.

Nick took a deep breath and let it out slowly, gazing up at the sky. He shook his head. "No."

"Do you want to now?"

Nick cocked his head and scrutinized Kelly. Kelly grew considerably warmer as he watched Nick's eyes. Nick began to smile. His voice was lower and full of gravel when he answered. "Definitely."

Kelly swallowed hard and flushed. "Likewise."

The mischievous smile Nick responded with only made Kelly want to squirm. Goddamn, why had he never noticed how sexy Nick was when he grinned like that?

Nick licked his lips to wipe the smirk away and looked down at his hands. "So, you're wondering why."

"Yes."

"Does it matter?" Nick asked neutrally.

Kelly held his breath, considering. "Yes?"

"Okay."

Kelly smiled. Of course Nick would just accept it and proceed to try to find a solution. That was the way Nick was. That was the way they both were, to an extent, which often led to a distinct absence of gnashing of teeth and wailing between them when problems arose.

Nick gripped the railing with both hands. "Part of the excitement of attraction is knowing it's reciprocated, right?"

Kelly nodded. "We found out last night that we, um . . ."

"Reciprocate," Nick provided. They both grinned, meeting each other's eyes. The warmth and excitement of new attraction were bolstered by years of history. Years of camaraderie. Years of comfort. It was something entirely new, and it was something that just felt right.

Kelly inhaled sharply as the realization hit him. "This would be so easy."

Nick bit his lip, not responding. Instead he reached out and ran his fingers over Kelly's wrist.

"God, O, this would be *so easy*," Kelly said more emphatically. He moved carefully and leaned on the railing beside Nick. "You and me? Just . . . can you imagine?"

Nick gave that a low whistle and nodded. He raised his head, the smile gone. "I *can* imagine. I'm trying not to, though."

"Why?"

"A few weeks ago you almost died," Nick said, his voice gone rough. "Your view of the world has shifted."

"How do you know?"

"Because I've almost died a couple times, Kels. I remember what it's like to . . . to realize you're still here when you shouldn't be."

Kelly swallowed hard and nodded. He remembered the weeks of desperate searching when Ty and Nick had gone missing. He remembered how it had felt, trying to accept that they were gone and he'd never been able to say good-bye, to tell them what they both meant to him. He'd written letters to their families. They'd never been mailed, thank God, but he'd still sobbed while writing them.

He remembered the day he'd seen a transport truck roll into camp with Ty and Nick laid out in the back, thinking they were dead. He and Owen had climbed into that truck faster than the lieutenant had been able to order them away. Kelly'd found the pulse at Nick's neck and wanted to throw up with relief.

His stomach lurched and he turned his hand over to grasp Nick's fingers. Nick squeezed Kelly's hand as if he knew what he was thinking, what he was recalling.

"Before last night, you'd never even considered *kissing* another man, much less whatever's in your head now," Nick continued.

"That's not entirely true. I'd thought about it. Just never seriously. Or while sober."

"Still. You're in uncharted territory. It *would* be easy. Us."

Kelly looked up.

"Just sex is one thing. I think we could manage that and not lose each other. But talking about anything else right now would be . . ."

"Crazy?" Kelly asked.

Nick smiled.

"You're right."

"I know," Nick said with a grin.

Kelly barked a laugh. "Shut up. Hear me out, though. Okay?"

Nick picked up Kelly's hand and held it, his fingers playing with Kelly's. He nodded.

Kelly tore his eyes away from their hands to examine Nick's profile. "We know each other better already than we could ever hope to know anyone else. Our pasts, our hopes and fears, all our secrets. We've already shared all that. We know we're compatible. Hell, we even know we can live together."

"That's debatable," Nick mumbled. He gave Kelly a sly grin.

"Shut up. At least you already know all my bad habits, right?"

"Like licking the germs off a spoon and putting it back in the drawer?"

"I only did that once," Kelly mumbled. "But you know I love M&M's in my pancakes. I know you eat French fries with ranch instead of ketchup and that you steal the marshmallows out of Lucky Charms when you think no one's looking."

Nick began to laugh.

"You know I squeeze the toothpaste from the middle, and I know you used to go behind me with one of those tube squeezers every morning and fix it so no one else would get mad at me. And I know you wake up in the middle of the night sometimes so terrified you don't even recognize your own name. And I know the only people you'll let spend the night in bed with you are people you know can fight you off if you try to hurt them."

Nick's eyes had gone wider, and he fought to swallow as Kelly spoke. He looked vulnerable, something Nick rarely seemed, and Kelly wanted to wrap him in a hug.

"Sometimes I wake up screaming too," Kelly whispered. "But I never have when I was sharing a bed with you. And after last night we know there's a whole lot to work with below the belt, you know what I mean?"

Nick nodded and looked down, smiling. Kelly reached for him, grabbing his chin and forcing him to meet his eyes to make sure Nick heard him.

"This could work out pretty nice for both of us, Nicko. I've never been with anyone where it was so easy so fast. Where it felt like home. But you've always been home to me."

Nick's eyes caught the sunlight and almost made Kelly forget what he'd been saying.

"Kelly," Nick tried. His voice faltered, and he had to stop to swallow.

"I've already got more with you than I've ever had anywhere," Kelly said in a rush, trying to beat Nick to whatever he'd been about to say. He took a deep breath to calm himself. "And after last night?"

"It would be easy." Nick sighed and ran his thumb along Kelly's knuckles.

Kelly dropped his hand away from Nick's chin. "But you're still going to say no, aren't you?"

"I will never say no to you," Nick said, his voice soft.

"Is it this guy you're not dating?"

"Aidan," Nick provided, trying not to laugh. "We're not dating, but not for lack of trying."

Jealousy spiked so quickly that Kelly barely recognized the feeling. "I don't understand what that means."

"He's a fireman. Our first date, a warehouse caught fire," Nick explained. "He left me at the fire station. Do you have any idea the rivalry between cops and firefighters in Boston? I'm surprised I didn't end up duct-taped to the fire pole or something."

Kelly began to laugh, biting his lip to stop himself.

"The second first date, there was a triple homicide and I had to leave him sitting in my squad car for two hours. He got into the back to take a nap, and didn't realize the doors would lock behind him."

Kelly began to laugh despite how much he hated the idea of Nick dating anyone. Nick chuckled softly, shaking his head.

"We decided that 'dates' weren't good for the city after that, so we didn't try again."

"So you're basically fuck buddies."

Nick shrugged noncommittally, glancing away.

"So why are you saying no to me?"

Nick sighed loudly. "What I'm saying right now is wait."

Kelly's shoulders slumped. The disappointment was sharper than he'd expected. "Wait?"

"Wait. Until you're better. Until all of this isn't shiny and new. Until life feels normal for you again."

Kelly made a disgusted sound. "What's normal anyway?"

Nick chuckled. "I wouldn't be any kind of friend if I let you make decisions with a bottle of painkillers and a fresh bullet hole in your back."

The disappointment spiked, but Kelly should have known Nick would be reasonable and levelheaded. Nick was the first person willing to jump, but he'd also be the one making sure you had your parachute on. "What about you?" Kelly asked, his voice hoarse.

"What about me?"

"What will you do while I'm getting better and rubbing the shine off things?"

Nick smiled crookedly. "Hopefully I'll be getting rubbed a little too."

They both laughed, not looking away from each other. Kelly liked how bold Nick was; it was completely at odds with his nonchalant attitude. He'd seen Nick in action, of course, but he'd never been the target. He understood the attraction now. Completely understood.

He moved impulsively, grabbing for Nick's shirtfront and pulling him into a kiss. Nick moved with him, turning into him. He picked Kelly up by the backs of his thighs and set him on the railing, crowding in close between his legs as they kissed. Kelly didn't even have time to register how weird it felt to be manhandled. He didn't worry about falling backward off the railing. It was natural to trust Nick to hold him, to wrap his arms around Nick's neck and squeeze his knees against Nick's hips.

The kiss was rough and consuming, just like Nick. Just like everything Kelly loved about Nick.

Nick took Kelly's face in both hands when he pulled away. He pressed his forehead to Kelly's cheek, his breath harsh against Kelly's neck. "Put your feet on the ground," he said, voice gone hard. He gripped Kelly's arms to keep him from tilting backward, but he stepped away too.

Kelly fought the urge to grab him and stop him from backing off.

"We need to take that walk," Nick grumbled.

"I'd rather climb the stairs."

Nick smiled weakly. Kelly gave him a small tug, but Nick resisted. He didn't break eye contact, but he looked like he desperately wanted to. He shook his head instead. "I was wrong, I can't do this."

"Nick."

"I'm serious, Kels. I don't want to hurt you."

"Baby, I got two Percocet in me, I'm untouchable right now!" Kelly drawled, giving Nick's arm a tug.

Nick put a hand over his eyes. "Please don't remind me that you lack clear decision-making skills right now."

"What?"

"Percocet. That's not what I meant and you know it."

"Is this about you and Aidan?"

"No. Sort of. No," Nick stammered. He ran his hand over his face. "I just, this feels dangerous to me, Doc."

"I know what this is," Kelly grumbled.

Nick laughed bitterly. "I doubt that, because even I don't know what this is. So let's just leave it at this and go take a walk." Nick moved away, leaving Kelly leaning against the railing trying to catch his breath.

"This is your fear of commitment cropping up, huh? Isn't that usually like a fifth date thing for you?"

Nick stopped short and turned to face him.

"I call bullshit," Kelly said. He crossed his arms over his chest stubbornly.

"Are you really psychoanalyzing me right now?"

"I know the gears in your head by name, bud. You're not going to pull any of this shit with me."

Nick worked his jaw and looked away.

"What are you really afraid of?" Kelly asked.

Nick glared at him, his eyes blazing briefly before he calmed again. "You know exactly what I'm afraid of."

"The same thing that made you keep your mouth shut about Ty all those years?"

Nick's jaw jumped as he clenched his teeth.

"It'll never happen," Kelly said calmly. "If we try this and it doesn't work, that's it. There's no drama between us. It won't hurt us. It won't hurt our friendship."

Nick looked up at the sky, taking a deep breath. "Kels, I'm begging you to stop."

"Nick," Kelly tried as he moved closer. "It's me. I know why you're panicking right now. I know—"

"Don't," Nick growled.

Kelly took a deep breath and went for it anyway. "You're afraid of this moving past the 'just sex' point, right? You're afraid it might be something special, because that's sure as hell what it felt like last night. You're scared."

Nick put both hands on his hips and lowered his head, nodding. "Okay," he said, then turned and stalked toward the door, disappearing inside.

Kelly sighed heavily, left alone on his deck as the breeze plucked at the hem of his shirt and ruffled his hair. "Well, that went well."

Nick sat in a swing on the front deck, his feet propped on the railing, an unlit cigarette in his hand. He'd wanted to simply bolt, to get out and clear his head for a few hours, but even angry he wasn't willing to leave Kelly alone. And since the cabin consisted of one open room downstairs and the loft bedroom, there was nowhere to run and hide. So he'd gone to the front deck and planted himself there for a few hours. Kelly had left him alone.

Nick had to smile. Just the fact that Kelly knew to leave him alone was something. He could almost forgive him for calling him out like he had.

He heard Kelly coming to the door, and he turned his head. "You need help?"

"No, I'm good," Kelly answered when he pushed past the screen door. He shuffled closer, holding his hand to his chest. He stopped at Nick's side and stared off at the setting sun. "I'm steadier if I don't take the pain pills."

"Yeah, but then you're in pain."

Kelly shrugged. "It takes some of the fear out of it. Being able to feel it all the way through. I'm realizing I've been babying myself for no reason."

Nick peered up at him. He brought the cigarette to his mouth and sucked on the filter. He hadn't smoked a cigarette in almost twenty years. But he still liked the way they felt in his hands, the ritual of bringing one to his lips, the way the tobacco smelled.

Kelly finally looked down at him. "Phantom smoking, huh?"

Nick smiled weakly, shrugging.

Kelly snickered and sat. "You know what the squids used to call you behind your back when you'd do that?"

"Ghost lighter," Nick answered, beginning to smile more. Kelly laughed. Nick handed the cigarette to him, and he put it in his mouth and sucked on the filter like Nick had done, then handed it back.

Nick stared at the cigarette for a long moment. He'd started smoking at twelve. He'd been eighteen when he'd met Ty, and the man had almost instantly broken him of it. He hadn't shamed him out of it or tried to subvert the habit, though. He'd simply stated the fact that craving a cigarette was one more weakness someone could exploit and that had been that.

A week later, Nick had been almost done with it. Almost. The only thing that remained was a craving for the action. It didn't matter if it was a cigarette, a straw, or a stick. He almost always had something in his mouth, like the toothpick Kelly had plucked from his lips that morning. It didn't matter. It was still a weakness, he supposed. One of his few. And Kelly knew the whole story.

"I could never break myself of it."

"We all have our vices," Kelly muttered.

"I'm sorry," Nick said under his breath. He glanced at Kelly, meeting his eyes. "I'm sorry."

Kelly shook his head. "Me too. I knew better. I shouldn't have poked at that."

"You're one of the only people who knows it's there to poke. I have to give you points for that." They stared at each other in the silence, neither compelled to speak or look away. Nick brought the cigarette to his mouth again, sucking in the faint taste of tobacco before handing it over to Kelly. "You ready for that walk now?"

"No." Kelly pulled a lighter out of his back pocket and lit the cigarette. He took a long drag, then exhaled the smoke in a stream that began to waft on the breeze. He grinned. "A hole shot in my lung, I was hoping you'd be able to see smoke come through the stitches," he said, snickering as he handed it back to Nick.

Nick smiled sadly, watching his companion in the dying light. He turned his attention to the glowing tip of the cigarette. He'd been a private the last time he'd smoked. He stared at it a little longer, then turned it over and ground the tip into the railing.

When he tore his attention away from it, Kelly was watching him. "You know what I always admired about you, Irish?"

"I can't imagine."

"You knew right from wrong."

Nick raised both eyebrows, smiling. "That's not exactly a huge feat."

"Yeah, it is. In our lives? The things we've been part of? Yeah, it is. Your moral compass always pointed the right way. And no matter what you wanted, you always followed where it led you. So if last night didn't feel right to you, I'll trust that."

Nick stared at him, trying to decipher the feeling the words gave him. He was both honored by Kelly's opinion of him and oddly disappointed. He shook his head. What scared him about last night wasn't that it had felt wrong. It had felt right. Really fucking right. And that was the core of his current problem. His moral compass was spinning.

Kelly took a deep, shaky breath. "But at the risk of pissing you off even more," he said, his face hard and his voice stern, "I'm going to say this again because I don't think you've heard it enough. I don't think you believe it."

Nick's entire body went cold. He held his breath, telling himself to let Kelly finish this time.

"You're a good man," Kelly whispered. "One of the best I've ever known. And if you're denying yourself a life with someone who loves you because you don't think you deserve it, then you're not as smart as I think you are. And if you're saying no to me because you're afraid, then you're a pussy."

Nick's lips twitched. "How long did you practice that before you came out here?"

"About an hour," Kelly answered, breaking into a smile. "Was it good? How'd I do?"

Nick nodded. "It was good."

"You believe me?"

Nick inhaled deeply, butterflies churning in his stomach. "Yeah, I do."

"Do you believe me when I say I want the D?"

Nick choked back a laugh. He ran his fingers over his forehead, smiling crookedly. "Yeah, I do. This is the worst idea we've ever had."

Kelly's grin widened. "I agree. Want to go upstairs and get naked?"

"Kind of," Nick drawled.

"Want to not smoke another cigarette first?"

They both laughed. Their camaraderie had always been easy. Nick's inner composure fed off Kelly's outward calm, and Kelly's quirkiness fed off Nick's nonchalance. Kelly was probably right when he said there'd be no drama between them.

Kelly pulled himself out of his chair, moving closer to Nick. He slapped his shoulder and waved at him. "Scoot over."

Nick did, sliding to the far side of the swing to let Kelly settle beside him. He kept his hand on the back of the swing and Kelly leaned into the crook of his arm. It wasn't something they'd never done before, because Nick had a tendency to put his arm around whoever was sitting next to him regardless of who it was. But this time felt different. Everything about Kelly felt different now. Different, yet still familiar. Nick realized that would never change. What he was afraid of happening had already happened, and they would never be able to go back to what they'd been.

There was no retreat. Retreat, hell. The only option now was to move forward. They just needed to pick their path and stick to it.

"It's me you're dealing with," Kelly said, bringing Nick back to the present. "You don't have to hide shit from me, you know? You don't have to protect me from any part of you. I already know it all. And you know all of me."

Nick watched Kelly's profile, unable to tear his eyes away, unable to say anything.

Kelly pulled a blunt out of his pocket and held it up. "You still smoke these?"

Nick huffed, smirking. "Only when I know I'm not going back to work."

Kelly put it between his lips and lit up. The tip glowed as he took a long drag, then he rested his head against Nick's arm and closed his eyes. Nick took the blunt from his fingers, his eyes not leaving Kelly's face.

Kelly released the smoke in a slow stream, not moving. "I won't hurt you. And I know you won't hurt me. So fuck it, Irish, let's try this."

Nick took a hit and pondered Kelly's words. They passed it between them several more times, watching the sun set against the mountain peaks.

"We'll never be the same," Nick finally said. He needed to know that Kelly had thought this through, that he was aware of what the morning light would reveal.

Kelly barked a laugh. "We pole-vaulted over that last night."

Nick leaned closer, curling his arm around Kelly's shoulders. He brushed his nose along Kelly's neck, just behind his ear. Kelly inhaled sharply. The goose bumps rose on his arms and he turned his head into the contact.

Nick brushed his lips against Kelly's cheek.

"You really think this can go bad?" Kelly whispered. "When everything about it feels so fucking good?"

Nick breathed in deeply, truly giving the question thought rather than letting his gut reaction take over. "Only if we let it, I guess," he finally decided, his lips moving against Kelly's cheek.

"Do you trust me?" Kelly asked.

"You know I do." Nick gripped Kelly's chin, pulling his face until their lips met. Kelly immediately leaned into him, groaning as Nick's teeth scraped over his lip, as their tongues met and teased. The kiss was so consuming that Nick got lost in it, all his senses absorbed by it. It was still crazy to think this was the Doc he was kissing, to think he was getting turned on just sitting here and kissing *Kelly*. He would have to pole-vault over that hurdle too, because this was too damn good to pass up just because it was weird.

He sucked Kelly's bottom lip between his one last time before ending the kiss and pulling back with a gasp for air.

Kelly licked at his lips, forcing his eyes open to meet Nick's. "Okay, see that? That's good stuff. I think we should do more of that."

"Remember what I told you about thinking?" Nick asked, voice lowered.

Kelly's breath hitched. "How could I forget?"

Nick released his hold on Kelly's chin, running his fingers up to brush along his cheekbone. Kelly's eyes were a shade close to blue, with hints of green and gray depending on what reflected in them. Nick had always been fascinated by Kelly's eyes. He'd maybe even fantasized about kissing him a few times, but he'd never lusted after him.

Not until now.

"I'm going to be honest with you right now," he said, voice gruff. "I'm hard in my fucking jeans just thinking about what I could do to you."

Kelly chuckled, his eyes growing darker as they dilated. Nick couldn't stop looking into them.

"But we're going to have to be high or drunk or both the first few times we do this, because it's too fucking weird to kiss you otherwise."

Kelly nodded. "I agree to those terms."

"Good. You want to go upstairs and get fucked?"

Kelly stuffed the blunt back into his pocket and grabbed Nick's shoulder, using him to push himself off the swing. "Come on."

Nick began to laugh, moving slowly as Kelly tried to rush him. "How's your chest?"

"It pulls. But it doesn't hurt enough to refuse a second helping of last night, so come on."

Nick stared at him, letting the nerves settle a little more before Kelly pulled him to his feet. He took hold of Kelly's hips and stopped him before he could turn away, pulling their bodies together. Kelly had to tip his head back to meet Nick's eyes.

"It's just sex, right?" Nick whispered.

Kelly narrowed his eyes, then began to grin. "Don't punk out on me now, O'Flaherty."

Nick grunted as Kelly pushed away from him. "Those are my terms," he called after him.

"Come on," Kelly said, disappearing inside. "Let's go get stoned and fuck."

Nick watched him for a moment before shrugging and following. He trailed behind Kelly as he made his way up the stairs. Kelly had been right: he was much steadier without the painkillers. But he also moved slower and more gingerly. Nick was having second thoughts about this by the time he was halfway up the stairs. Kelly was obviously still in pain, and Nick knew exactly what kind of damage he could when he got worked up.

When he reached the head of the stairs, Kelly stood near the end of the bed, waiting with a tentative half smile on his face. "This feels like a prom date or something," he said.

Nick nodded, glancing around the loft bedroom with another flutter of nerves. "We've already altered our relationship with last night," he said. "We'll never get that back."

"I know," Kelly said softly.

"We can stop here and just go to sleep."

Kelly narrowed his eyes, a smile flitting across his lips. "You're going to look for the exit at every turn, aren't you?"

Nick huffed.

Kelly began to unbutton his shirt. "Well there ain't no exits on this ride, babe, 'cause I know all your tricks."

Nick grinned. He watched the slow reveal, something he'd rarely let himself linger over in the past. Kelly had some fucking incredible shoulders and arms, that much was for sure. And the rest of him might as well have been an amusement park, as fun as he was to explore. Nick would have to retrain his way of thinking if they were going to be fucking and he was actually allowed to leer now. He licked his lips, reaching up to pull at the buttons of his soft flannel shirt.

"From now on I'm just going to have to jump you, aren't I?" Kelly asked with a laugh. "Talking doesn't work on you, but getting naked does."

Nick tossed his shirt toward the nearby chair. Kelly let his own shirt drop to the floor.

"From now on?" Nick repeated.

"That's right."

"How long are we talking about here?"

"As long as we're happy?" Kelly suggested. His hands moved to the band of his sweatpants and shoved them down. He was growing hard just standing there with Nick's eyes on him. "As long as we're having fun. As long as you're not panicking because you think you're in a relationship."

Nick licked his lips again, blatantly watching as Kelly stepped out of his pants. Kelly spread his arms wide, inviting Nick to look. Inviting him to do a hell of a lot more than look.

"Isn't that how it's done?"

Nick shook his head and slowly moved toward Kelly, looking him up and down as he circled him.

"I'm not asking you to buy the milk, O'Flaherty, I just want you to grope the cow," Kelly said, trying to hide a sly smile by biting his lip.

Nick chuckled and stepped up behind him. He slid his hands over Kelly's waist, pulling their bodies together. Kelly hummed, and Nick bent to kiss the back of Kelly's shoulder.

Kelly turned his head, his nose brushing Nick's hair. "Come on, Lucky. You think I can't feel how much you want this?"

Nick inhaled sharply, rubbing his hard cock against Kelly's ass. One hand gripped Kelly's hip while the other dragged up his body, avoiding the new scar on his chest and finally coming to rest just under Kelly's neck. He could feel the rise and fall of Kelly's increasingly labored breathing.

"I'd give anything to fuck you tonight," Nick hissed in Kelly's ear. Before he knew what he was doing, his hand had ventured higher and tightened at Kelly's throat. His forefinger and thumb rested on the defined edges of Kelly's jaw.

"Why won't you?" Kelly gasped. His pulse raced under Nick's fingertips.

Nick closed his eyes. "I told you once. I'm not going to hurt you." He kissed Kelly's shoulder again, then his neck. Kelly groaned, vibrating Nick's palm. Nick tugged him, turning them around and walking Kelly a few steps until he was facing the wall. He took care to be gentle when he pushed Kelly against it, still holding him by his neck and hip.

Kelly's hands came up to press against the wall and he blew an unsteady stream of air out. He was trembling.

He put his lips to Kelly's ear and hummed, the sound low and rumbling. He closed his eyes and thrust his hips against Kelly's ass again, trying to be calm, trying to be gentle. He could imagine what it would be like to slide inside Kelly and make him writhe and scream, to take him on his knees. His grip tightened on Kelly's throat as he thought about it.

"Jesus Christ," Kelly gasped. "I don't know why I find this so fucking hot, but I do."

"Okay," Nick grumbled. "You're going to have to stop reminding me you've never done this before."

He forced Kelly's head to the side and strained to be able to kiss him over his shoulder. Kelly growled against his mouth, nipping at his lip and tongue, his body pushing back against Nick's as he tried to turn. Nick shoved him harder to the wall, tightening his grip. His bare chest pressed against Kelly's warm back. The denim of his jeans caught at Kelly's naked skin, his belt buckle digging in. He took his hand from Kelly's hip and fumbled with his belt and zipper.

"Yeah," Kelly breathed.

Nick shoved his jeans and boxers down just enough to free his cock, then reached down and guided it against the crack of Kelly's ass. Kelly's entire body tensed and he shoved up onto his toes to make him closer to Nick's height. Nick shivered as Kelly's reaction reverberated through him.

"I'm not going inside you," he hissed in Kelly's ear. Kelly nodded. "But I do plan on coming all over your ass, so buckle the fuck up."

Kelly groaned again and Nick pulled back on his chin, forcing Kelly to look up at the ceiling. He pushed Kelly's entire body against the wall, thrusting his hips and dry-humping him between his legs.

Kelly made a growling, whimpering sound. "Are you sure you won't fuck me?"

Nick grunted, pressing his face against Kelly's cheek. "I'd wreck you."

"Sounds fun," Kelly said, choking on the words.

Nick closed his eyes. "We'll get there. Do you have condoms? Lube?" he asked, barely able to get the words out.

"Does it matter what kind?" Kelly asked. He was gritting his teeth and his eyes were closed.

"The kind you use when you get off."

"Drawer by the bed."

Nick stepped back, putting his hand between Kelly's shoulder blades. "Stay."

Kelly nodded, resting his forehead against the wall. He reached down to palm himself. "Do we really need condoms?" he asked.

Nick glanced back at him as he rummaged through the drawer. "Less mess."

"Messy is hot as hell." Kelly still hadn't opened his eyes, and he was stroking himself languidly. "I trust you if you say we don't need them."

Nick's stomach flipped. He'd never once been with someone he would trust at their word for going without a cover. But Kelly was different, and Nick didn't even give it a second thought. He dropped the condom back into the drawer and returned to press against Kelly's back. He reached around him, replacing Kelly's hand with his own to stroke Kelly's hard cock a few times. Then he gripped Kelly's wrist and brought it back out, shoving it hard against the wall.

Their fingers twined together.

Nick kissed at Kelly's neck. "Do me a favor, okay?" he whispered. Kelly nodded. "Don't come until I'm ready to swallow it, you hear me?"

Kelly grunted and made another whimpering sound, but he nodded.

"I don't care if I'm in the middle of shooting my load inside that sweet ass of yours, you start to come, you shove your dick down my throat any way you can."

"Got it," Kelly gasped. He grinned and rested his head back on Nick's shoulder, his eyes still closed. "I got it. Holy fuck."

Nick smiled and filled one hand with lubricant. He dropped the bottle and took himself in hand, stroking and covering his cock in lube.

He bent his head to kiss Kelly's shoulder. Then he dragged his teeth over the skin, biting down. Kelly moaned and pushed his ass back against Nick's cock.

"You like that?" Nick asked.

"I don't know. I'm no longer in control of my ass."

Nick laughed. He took his cock and slid the head between Kelly's ass cheeks. "That's because your ass is mine right now," he growled, then bit down again on Kelly's shoulder and rocked his hips harder. His slick cock slid easily, gliding against Kelly's ass.

Kelly pushed back, shimmying his hips. Nick let Kelly's hand go and grabbed his neck again, yanking his head back so he could kiss and bite and suck at his collarbone and jaw and neck. The sounds Kelly made with each nip were intoxicating.

"Goddamn, I want to eat you alive," Nick snarled, pulling a desperate moan from Kelly. Kelly's knees were going weak, though, and he seemed to be using all his strength to keep his chest from hitting the wall. Nick worked harder to hold him up, reminding himself to be gentler as he worked his hips, seeking friction for his thrusts. He reached around Kelly with his slick hand and palmed his cock, beginning to stroke him, his movements forcing Kelly to fuck his hand.

Kelly rose on his toes again. He exhaled in a gust. Nick shoved Kelly's head to the side and their lips sought each other out, sucking and biting, their tongues lapping. Nick found the tight ring of muscle at Kelly's ass with the head of his cock, pushing at it with a careful thrust.

Kelly moaned wantonly, and the sound went straight to Nick's throbbing cock. Kelly's jumped in Nick's hand, the tip leaking against his thumb.

"If I beg, will you shove that into me?" Kelly asked.

"No," Nick ground out. He thrust harder though, pressing at those muscles, making Kelly think he could enter him. There was no way he'd force himself past those tense muscles, though, not for the first time.

"Jesus Christ, Nick," Kelly gasped. His hands splayed against the wall.

Nick moaned, pressing his face into Kelly's neck. He took advantage of the tension pouring off Kelly's body, of the chance to let Kelly feel Nick's cock pressing at those muscles.

Their panting breaths mingled together. Kelly's strangled gasps were loud in Nick's ears. He pushed his ass back, obviously liking the feeling and wanting more. With some patience and preparation, Kelly was going to be one hell of an entertaining bottom. Nick could imagine exactly what it would be like to stretch him out on a bed and lay into him.

"Kels," Nick ground out, desperately fighting back his orgasm.

"Come on, Nick!" Kelly shouted. He reached back and dug his fingernails into Nick's ribs, breaking the skin as he dragged them. Nick shouted and tightened his grip on Kelly's neck, pulling his whole body away from the wall and then slamming him into it as he came.

Kelly talked the whole way through, mumbling to him, begging him, groaning and moaning. Nick held to him as they both gasped and grunted, as his cum spurted between Kelly's legs and against his ass.

"Jesus fucking Christ that feels good," Kelly finally panted.

Nick pushed away from him, taking hold of his shoulder and turning him to press his back against the wall. Kelly was biting his lip, his eyes fluttering as he tried and failed to keep them open. Nick stepped close and kissed him, diving into it. Kelly's hands tangled in his hair.

Nick growled into the languid kiss. All sense of urgency had leaked out of both of them, and Nick's palm was covered in cum that wasn't his. He pulled away from the kiss. "You came, didn't you?"

Kelly began to laugh, curling around Nick and pressing their bodies closer.

"Jackass," Nick muttered against his lips.

Kelly stretched out on the lounger on the small balcony outside his bedroom. The stars winked overhead. The moon shone down, bright on his bare skin. It was cool enough that Nick had gone back inside for a blanket, because neither of them was willing to get dressed again.

Nick's cum was drying between his legs. He'd refused to clean up because he wanted to feel it there. It was a singularly odd sensation, but Kelly was digging it. In fact, it was sexy as hell. He was all for new experiences, after all.

He was also pretty sure there was going to be a handprint on his neck. Bite marks on his shoulder. Jesus Christ, that was hot. And he'd actually been compelled to put Neosporin on Nick's ribs where he'd drawn blood.

He heard Nick bang into something and cuss it up and down before stumbling out onto the balcony. Kelly snickered as Nick wrapped the blanket around his shoulders and cursed the table one more time.

"I'm pretty sure that wasn't there before," Nick grumbled.

Kelly laughed harder. "I'm pretty sure it was."

"Shut up."

"You're high."

"Oh, look at the pothead calling the kettle names," Nick said in a singsong voice as he settled onto the wide chaise beside Kelly. They both laughed harder. Nick pulled the blanket over them, and the warmth of his naked body against Kelly's was so welcome that Kelly turned into it. A moment later Nick had his arm under Kelly's neck, giving him a cushion to rest his head on, and he wrapped his arm around Kelly to pull him closer. Their temples pressed together as they both looked up at the night sky.

"Jesus," Nick muttered. "Even out on the water the stars aren't like this."

Kelly hummed in agreement and passed Nick the blunt they'd started on earlier. Nick brought out the lighter he'd retrieved with the blanket.

Kelly wasn't sure he should have found it sexy to watch Nick light the thing. He'd seen him do it a hundred times before. They were the only members of Sidewinder who appreciated the intricacies of herbal refreshment, so they'd done this together a lot over the years, sneaking away and sitting under the stars to share a hit. But this was the first time Kelly had ever appreciated Nick's form.

He was falling hard and fast and he didn't care why or how. Wrapped up in this blanket under the stars, he could admit that. He always fell fast, though, and he knew Nick. Nick could smell someone falling in love from a mile away. Kelly had seen him bolt like a scared whitetail deer more than once, so he'd have to be careful.

Nick took a long drag as he stared up at the sky. His body was relaxing, settling into the lounger and into Kelly. He turned his head, placing the burning tip of the blunt into his mouth. He reached for Kelly's chin, pulling him until their lips met. Kelly slid his fingertips against Nick's cheek as they shotgunned the hit. Nick blew smoke into his mouth as their bodies curled together, then he took the blunt and pulled it away, stealing a languid kiss before Kelly got a chance to exhale.

They began to laugh even as the kiss continued. Nick pulled away, and Kelly turned his head to blow smoke into the night, laughing harder.

They lay curled together, sharing the blunt until it was gone and getting higher than the stars they watched, drawing warmth from each other when they probably should have been inside.

"This is good, Kels," Nick finally murmured.

Kelly turned his head to peer at Nick in the moonlight. He was staring at the sky, the same way he always did when they'd wander off and lie down somewhere and get high.

Kelly grinned. "I grow it myself in the woods out back."

Nick began to laugh, the sound kicking Kelly off into a fit of giggling too. Nick pulled Kelly closer. He turned his head, pressing his face against Kelly's. "That's not what I meant."

Their lips met, and before Kelly knew what was happening, they were curling around each other, kissing more, their legs tangling, their bodies aligning in ways Kelly had never realized they could.

"This *is* good," Kelly whispered. "What do we do about it?"

"Wing it," Nick growled. "It's what we've always done."

Kelly nodded. "You promise to fuck me eventually?"

He felt Nick smile into the kiss. "Promise."

When Kelly woke, the sun was streaming through the loft of the cabin and he was alone in bed. Again. He glanced around. Music was playing downstairs. On the table beside his bed was a bottle of water and his pills all lined in a row, waiting to be taken. There was also a packet of string cheese. A note was propped against the lamp, telling him to call for help before he tried to get out of bed, and to eat the cheese before taking his pills.

Kelly laughed and disregarded the note in every way, throwing his covers off and using the edge of the mattress to pull himself out of bed. He had to sit and gather his strength before he was able to push himself to stand, and once he was up he immediately regretted his intense meeting with the wall last night. But he padded into the bathroom, proud to have done it without having to call for help.

A quick examination in the mirror showed prominent bruises under his chin and around his neck. That was good, he supposed, it meant they weren't too deep. He also had several red welts where he remembered Nick's teeth digging in on his shoulder and neck. He found he didn't care. In fact, he was as proud of those battle injuries as he was of the rest.

He took care of business, giving himself one more look in the mirror before stepping back into the bedroom. Nick was sitting cross-legged on the bed, eating a piece of toast and scrolling through something on his iPad.

"Morning, Irish," Kelly said, his voice hoarse and scratchy.

"You think I can't hear you moving around from downstairs?" Nick asked without looking up from what he was reading.

"Are you getting crumbs in the bed?" Kelly asked.

Nick nodded without looking up from what he was reading. "Sheets need washing anyway," he said as he chewed. He finished what he was doing and raised his head, his eyes raking Kelly up and down as he set the iPad aside.

Kelly shrugged. He shuffled back to the bed, and Nick moved to help him. Kelly tried to swat him away, but Nick easily grabbed his hand and wrapped an arm around him. His chest fluttered. Nick's scent now reminded him of everything good in the world. He turned at the edge of the bed, looking into Nick's eyes and putting his arm around Nick's neck so Nick could help him sit. Nick's arms tightened around him.

He leaned in and kissed Kelly gently. Kelly could feel him smiling into the kiss, and it made him grin too.

Nick finally let him go, leaving them both gasping. "Good morning."

"Pretty spectacular one."

Nick helped him sit, his hands lingering when they probably didn't need to. Kelly gritted his teeth with the pull in his chest. Mornings were always worse because the painkillers in his system were running low and his body was stiff and stubborn. It was also a little embarrassing not to be able to sit down by himself, but he supposed that was what happened when a bullet tore through you and then you decided you were tougher than your painkillers.

Nick piled the pillows for him, and Kelly rested against the headboard, watching Nick unabashedly.

"You feeling okay?" Nick asked, and the gravel in his voice sent a shiver up Kelly's spine.

"Not as good as I was last night, unfortunately."

Nick's fingers were gentle as he brushed them over Kelly's neck. "How about you take your pills instead of trying to prove how tough you are?"

Kelly snorted.

Nick moved the breakfast tray he'd brought up so it was beside Kelly on the bed, making sure everything was within arm's reach, then rounded the bed and crawled into the other side, sitting against the headboard with his iPad.

Kelly crunched down on a piece of bacon. After living together for five years while they'd been stationed at Lejeune, Nick knew exactly how crispy he liked his bacon. He knew a lot of things. Kelly waved his bacon at the iPad. "Anything interesting going on?"

Nick nodded, still chewing. "Ty sent a message earlier saying he was heading back to Baltimore. Digger's convinced he's being watched by the CIA. And Owen came out of it smelling like roses and got a fucking Easter bonus. Asshole."

Kelly chuckled.

"I've been suspended," Nick added after a moment, still smiling at the iPad as he checked his email.

"What?"

"Suspended without pay until they straighten out the warrant for my arrest in Louisiana," Nick explained, beginning to laugh.

"That's bullshit," Kelly muttered.

Nick shrugged it off. "It's the second time I've been in custody in the last year, I'd suspend me too."

He laughed again and placed the iPad aside, turning to look at Kelly instead. "You okay?"

"Yeah," Kelly said with a nod, taking stock mentally. He nodded again. "Yeah, I'm good."

Nick hesitated briefly, then said, "I've got to write up a steaming pile of bullshit for my captain telling him why I shouldn't be fired."

"Go do it," Kelly said, laughing despite the underlying worry that Nick might actually lose his job.

"You sure?"

"Yeah, I'm good. I'm going to rest for a bit."

Nick narrowed his eyes skeptically.

"I'll call if I need help," Kelly assured him.

Nick gave him a brief kiss and rolled out of bed, taking his iPad downstairs. Kelly let his mind drift, thinking of Nick, thinking of their past together and the probability of them having a future. It was sudden and it was different, but Kelly still couldn't see a flaw in it. So what if Nick was famously afraid to move a romantic relationship past the fuck buddies stage? So what if Kelly'd never been with a guy before? Or even been attracted to a guy before.

He'd always acknowledged beauty in other men, but again, he'd never felt attraction. What if it really was the narcotics he'd been on the past few weeks? What if it was the near-death experience and Nick emerging as his caretaker? What if Nick was right and this was just a situational thing? What if the shine rubbed off?

What if they looked up in a week or a month and found that they'd permanently altered the shape of their friendship, a friendship Kelly valued more than anything in the world, all for the whim of a man on the brink of death and high on Percocet?

What if Kelly actually convinced Nick this was a good idea, and got past those defenses Nick had worked his whole life building up, only to decide it was the wrong thing after all? It would crush Nick.

Just the thought made Kelly nauseous. They were already on a slippery slope as it was; he needed to be damn sure they could take one more step without the whole cliff giving way.

When he looked up, he remembered he was alone. Nick had music playing low downstairs, obviously thinking it would cover the sounds of him muttering to himself so Kelly would rest. But Kelly couldn't rest. He needed to solidify this in his mind so he'd stop panicking. He called out for Nick, and soon he heard Nick's footsteps coming up the steps.

"I think I need to watch some gay porn," he told Nick as soon as the man reached the top.

Nick stopped short, eyes wide. A look of pure confusion passed over his face before he nodded and turned to head back down the steps. "I'll get the iPad."

Kelly was eating his cold bacon when Nick returned, iPad in hand.

"Am I to assume this is you trying to test if you're actually attracted to men instead of just being a horny stoner?" Nick asked as he crawled into the bed and propped the iPad between them.

"Something like that."

"What outcome are we hoping for here?" Nick asked as he tapped at the screen.

Kelly gazed at his profile. Nick glanced at him, returning Kelly's smirk with one of his own.

"I'm hoping I find watching a guy take it in the ass just as hot as I find the memory of you that night in San Diego," Kelly finally decided. "Or last night. Or the night before. Or just the thought of you doing to me what you did to that girl."

Nick was still looking at him sideways, but a flush began to appear on his cheeks.

Kelly swallowed hard, growing warmer. "You remember that night?"

"Yeah, I do."

"You . . . you were, um . . . impressive."

"I knew you were watching," Nick murmured.

"Exhibitionist."

"Voyeur."

Kelly laughed. He took the iPad from Nick's hands and pressed play on the video Nick had found. It wasn't a full video, just a free sample of something, so it started right in the middle of the act. The sound blasted through the quiet cabin. Kelly held the iPad at arm's length, cocking his head and frowning as he watched one man ram into another mercilessly, both of them contorting into unnatural positions. Nick leaned against the headboard beside him, but he didn't take his eyes off the video. There was a lot of moaning and slapping and what looked like some very advanced yoga poses, and by the time the five-minute video ended, Kelly wasn't certain it had done much for him.

He flopped the iPad into his lap and sighed.

"Nothing, huh?" Nick asked, sounding amused. Kelly shook his head. Nick reached for the iPad and clicked it off. "I tend to like the amateur ones myself."

Kelly glanced at him, his cock showing interest at the mere thought of Nick getting off to amateur porn.

"They're more real, less acrobatics," Nick explained, meeting Kelly's eyes without flinching. Kelly found it harder to breathe when Nick smiled mischievously. "Real people who are really attracted to each other. It's sexier. Sometimes just the roll of the hips is all it takes for me."

Kelly swallowed hard. "You realize what you just said got me harder than five minutes of watching two people fuck."

Nick smiled slowly.

"You are a devious asshole, you know that?"

"I do."

Kelly barked a laugh. "Is it possible to just be attracted to *one* guy, instead of *all* guys?"

"I don't know, Kels, anything's possible. You're not attracted to *all* women, are you?"

"Not really."

"There you go."

"I'm so confused," Kelly said with a sigh.

They sat side by side in the bed, looking at each other speculatively. Nick finally shrugged and smiled. He shifted and wrapped his arm around Kelly's shoulders, pulling gently until they were both reclining against the headboard.

"You know what I think?" Nick rumbled in Kelly's ear.

Kelly closed his eyes and leaned into Nick, smirking.

"I think you're thinking too hard. And I know why you're doing it."

"You do?"

"The same reason I am. You don't want to hurt me because you're my friend."

Kelly closed his eyes. Nick had the damnedest way of making things seem simple sometimes.

"Take your time figuring it out, Kels. I'll be here."

Kelly wasn't sure if it was the Percocet hitting him or Nick's simple promise that caused the warmth spreading through his chest. "You'd do that? You'd wait for me to figure things out?"

Nick began to grin. "I got no one better to do."

Kelly laughed despite trying not to. "What about that guy? What was his name? The fireman?"

Nick cleared his throat and loosened his hold on Kelly's shoulders. "Aidan. Like I said, that's been pretty casual. And . . . if there's something here with you?" He looked up and into Kelly's eyes. "How could I pass that up?"

Kelly caught his breath, staring into Nick's eyes and trying to decipher the heavy feeling in his chest. Nick drifted his knuckles over Kelly's cheekbone, and soon enough their lips met.

Something about the combination of gruff no-nonsense and tender attention was hitting buttons Kelly had never known he possessed. He could hear hints of the staff sergeant giving orders in Nick's words, but they were blunted by caresses full of adoration and mischief. It was a heady mixture, and it was signature Nick O'Flaherty. It was everything Kelly had always loved about Nick. His brusque leadership under fire—"Get your fat Navy ass down before I blow it off!"—and the warmth of his friendship in times of peace, all boiled down in this moment to a word and a gesture.

Kelly grabbed the front of Nick's shirt. Nick looked down at his hand, smiling when he met Kelly's eyes again.

"I don't care why or how," Kelly grunted. "I like this. I like seeing you like this. I like . . . I like thinking of you like this. I want more."

Nick opened his mouth to speak, but he seemed to struggle to say anything as his cheeks flushed.

"I'm serious, O."

"I know you are," Nick managed to say. He licked his lips and began to grin. Kelly's heart skipped a beat as he recognized the look in Nick's eyes. He had just decided to throw caution to the wind and follow Kelly into the fire, just like he'd done many times before. Damn the odds of getting hurt.

Kelly leaned and kissed him, wincing as his wound pulled with the movement. Nick pushed him back so he was against his nest of pillows again, still kissing him, his hands beginning to roam down Kelly's body.

But soon Nick grunted in annoyance and shoved away from him. "I just really can't do this properly until you're better."

Kelly grabbed for him and caught him by the collar. "Are you serious? How about improperly, then, because now I need it."

Nick fumbled behind him and grabbed the iPad, plopping it in Kelly's lap. "Watch more gay porn," he said as he tried to disengage his collar. "It'll calm you down."

Kelly released him and slapped him on the side of the head, but Nick took the punishment and then rolled away, out of Kelly's reach.

"Seriously?" Kelly cried.

"I don't want to get carried away and hurt you again, okay?" Nick said as he straightened his T-shirt. He looked and sounded sincere. "Because I will. Last night was bad enough. I mean Jesus, you look like you got strangled, and I fucking bled, man."

Kelly reached to the bedside table and grabbed a handful of bacon, chucking it at Nick with a laugh and a curse.

"Hey! I have to clean that up!"

"So get cleaning," Kelly said as he grabbed a handful of cold, soggy eggs.

"Don't," Nick warned with a point.

Kelly quirked an eyebrow.

"Don't you do it."

"Come give me a cuddle with a happy ending."

Nick was still pointing at him. "I will not be leveraged."

"Cuddle," Kelly said, waving his hand.

"I don't negotiate with terrorists!"

"Come on, Nicko, come give me a manly cuddle."

"Put down the eggs."

"Promise I'll get a cuddle?" Kelly asked.

Nick rolled his eyes. "Yes, just put down the eggs."

Kelly grinned triumphantly and plopped the eggs back onto the plate.

"Now you're disgusting, there's no way I'm touching you."

"I needed a shower today anyway," Kelly said with a shrug. Nick rounded the end of the bed, watching him warily. Kelly gave him a sly smile. "Will you help me?"

Nick pulled the covers back and bent over him, pressing a kiss to his lips before growling, "I end up with egg on me and you're on your own."

"Deal," Kelly managed. Nick hefted him out of bed, still kissing him, wrapping around him, growing more heated and pulling him closer. Before Kelly realized what he was doing, his hands were in Nick's hair, grabbing on so he could kiss him harder.

He felt Nick growl, the sound thrilling him down to his toes. He began to smile, laughing and desperately trying not to. "I'm sorry," he tried sincerely. He began to laugh harder, pulling his sticky hand away from Nick's hair. "I'm sorry I did it. And I'm even more sorry I'm laughing. I can't stop though."

Nick was silent for a moment, fuming. Then he shook his head and pulled Kelly back to him. "Fuck it," he snarled, delving into another kiss. He pulled Kelly toward the bathroom.

Kelly had to stand on his toes to wrap his arms around Nick's neck to kiss him. He didn't mind, though. It was kind of hot, actually, the height difference. Everything about Nick was hotter than the surface of the sun, and Kelly had to wonder why in the fuck he'd never noticed before. He pulled at the back of Nick's T-shirt, getting egg all over it. Nick stopped and yanked it over his head, pressing their bare chests together.

Kelly dragged his fingers across the oversized tattoo on Nick's shoulder, making him shiver.

"Gross," Nick groaned, then pulled Kelly through the bathroom door and into the shower stall. He pushed Kelly against the cold tiles, holding him there as he turned the shower nozzle away from them.

"You're still wearing your jeans," Kelly told him, smirking.

Nick's eyes were blazing when he met Kelly's, and it was quite obvious that he didn't care what got wet as long they were both naked and writhing when the water turned on. Nick grinned, and they both began to laugh. He quickly got out of his jeans and boxers, tossing them aside without breaking eye contact. There was something so intense just under the surface, Kelly was mesmerized. He'd seen it before, but only in battle. And last night. And the night before.

He shivered and raked his eyes up and down Nick's naked body. Even a decade after their last deployment, Nick hadn't changed much. He was still in peak physical condition, but his muscles were bulkier now. He'd injured his knee near the end, and he'd chosen to give up running, putting that energy into free weights instead.

Nick moved closer, pushing the tip of his nose along Kelly's cheek as he pressed their chest together gently. Over the sound of his blood rushing through his ears and Nick's harsh breath against his lip, Kelly heard the bell downstairs that signaled a car pulling up the gravel drive.

"What the fuck is that?" Nick ground out.

"Someone's here."

"You've got to be shitting me." Nick turned the water on quickly, ducking under it despite the fact that it was freezing cold, and washed the egg out of his hair. Then he stepped out of the shower, gathering his jeans up and stalking out of the bathroom.

Kelly was left alone as the water slowly warmed, mildly turned on and amused. He held his hand out to wash it clean, then stepped under the spray to at least wash the top layer of dirt off. He took his time getting dressed, because he didn't really have any other choice. And he took even more time getting down the stairs because tumbling down them didn't sound fun.

When he pushed through the front door, Nick was standing on the deck, shielding his eyes as he peered down the driveway. He'd thrown a flannel shirt on but hadn't buttoned it, and a gun was stuffed in the small of his back.

Nick's cell phone began to chime from the kitchen. The song was one Kelly recognized for Ty, but he didn't move to answer it. Someone coming down his driveway was unusual enough to warrant his undivided attention.

The car finally broke the ridge and came into sight, trailing dust and gravel. It was a government issue SUV.

"Son of a bitch," Nick hissed.

"Maybe it's a follow-up interview or something."

Nick squared his shoulders, rolling them and sort of unfurling. Kelly grinned. He'd always loved watching Nick prepare for battle. It was like watching a dog bristle. Kelly moved out onto the deck, standing shoulder to shoulder with him, waiting.

The car came to a stop where the driveway ended, next to Kelly's truck. The passenger door popped open, but it wasn't a man in a suit like Kelly expected. It was a Marine.

He peered up at Nick as the driver, another Marine, rounded the front of the car.

"Staff Sergeant Nicholas O'Flaherty?" the man questioned.

Nick stiffened as Kelly's blood ran cold.

"That's right."

The Marine came closer, standing at the bottom of the stairs. "It's an honor to meet you, Staff Sergeant." He waited a beat for Nick to respond, but when Nick didn't, he stepped closer, handing Nick a blue packet of papers. "Staff Sergeant, I'm here to inform you you've been recalled to active duty."

"What the hell?" Kelly blurted.

Nick was silent, reading the orders. He finally nodded, his jaw tight. "Thank you, Sergeant."

Kelly stared for a moment before taking a step forward. He had to grip the railing as he shook all over. "What about mine?"

The Marine hesitated, glancing at his companion.

Nick put a hand on Kelly's shoulder, squeezing. "Kels," he whispered.

"I'm sorry, sir," the Marine said. "We have no other orders to deliver."

"No, no, if the team is being called back, I'm going with them," Kelly shouted. "Kelly Abbott, check your goddamned orders again!"

Nick moved to stand in front of him, putting a hand on his hip as Kelly tried to go down the steps after the two Marines. "Kelly, stop. Stop!"

Kelly shoved at him, trying to break free, still shouting at the Marines. "You can't take my team without me! You can't send them back without me!"

Nick wrapped him up, glancing over his shoulder. "Go!" he shouted at the two men.

They hurried to obey, retreating to their SUV.

"Kelly, stop," Nick pleaded, his voice breaking as he held Kelly tighter. "Please, stop. Doc."

Kelly collapsed against him as the car pulled away. He lowered his head, resting it against Nick's shoulder as he let out an anguished shout. Nick was truly holding him up now. Kelly didn't care if he was standing or not. His team. His boys. He was supposed to be there with them.

"I'm sorry," Nick whispered. "I'm sorry, Doc."

Kelly lifted his head and shoved away from him, but Nick wouldn't let him go. He pulled him into a hug, placing Kelly's head under his chin and holding him tight.

"I know what you just did," Kelly whispered. He relaxed into Nick's protective embrace. Nicked hummed questioningly. "You weren't holding me back. You were holding me up."

Nick's arms tightened around him.

"So I wouldn't look weak in front of a Marine."

Nick rested his chin on Kelly's head, his hands grasping at Kelly's back. "You could never be weak. You carry the whole team with you."

Kelly groaned mournfully. The phone on the kitchen counter began to ring again.

"It's Ty," Nick said. "He was probably trying to warn us."

Kelly took a deep breath, trying to calm himself, trying to accept the crushing realization that everyone he loved was being called to war and he wasn't capable of going with them. "How long do you have?"

"Forty-eight hours," Nick said.

Kelly closed his eyes, holding his breath until he was almost lightheaded. He finally let it out and met Nick's eyes. Nick took Kelly's face in both hands. They stood in silence, staring into each other's eyes as both their cell phones rang and rang inside.

They converged in Charlotte, everyone flying in from around the country so they could report together as a team. They all knew it might be the last thing they did as a team, because there was no guarantee they'd be kept together once they were deployed.

Nick and Kelly sat together in one of the airport lounge areas, waiting for the others to arrive and join them. These would be their last moments alone together, the last chance they had to say what needed to be said. Nick couldn't think of a word that seemed adequate.

Kelly finally flopped his arm over Nick's shoulders. "When you're over there," he said, his voice pitched low. "I want you to remember you have unfinished business here, okay?"

Nick glanced at him, his heart in his throat when their eyes met.

Kelly's smile wavered, giving Nick a glimpse of the pain Kelly was trying to hide. "There's so much I want to say to you," Kelly whispered.

Nick's words were barely audible. "I know."

"I thought we'd have more time to figure this out, but . . . I'll wait for you to get back."

"Kels, you shouldn't do that."

Kelly smiled sadly. "I don't have anyone better to do," he drawled, echoing Nick's own words. Nick huffed, and Kelly leaned closer to press his forehead to Nick's temple. Nick patted his cheek. He turned his head and their lips found each other. It was almost physically painful to share that last kiss. When it ended, Nick couldn't breathe. He couldn't speak. He turned his head so they were once again leaning against each other, and he kept his hand on Kelly's cheek after he closed his eyes.

They sat that way in silence. Unmoving. Barely breathing. Nick's mind churned. He was nearly ill by the time someone touched him on the shoulder. He opened his eyes to find Ty and Zane standing in front of them, both looking as worn out and heartsick as Nick felt.

"Hey," Nick grunted.

Kelly looked up when he spoke. He stood and wrapped Ty up in a hug, holding on to him with the same kind of anguish he'd held on to Nick with last night. Nick met Zane's eyes, nodding at him. There really wasn't anything they could say. Nick stood to shake his hand, though, but Zane surprised him by stepping closer to hug him.

"Please bring him back alive," Zane whispered as he clung to Nick.

Nick nodded jerkily. "I promise."

Zane released him and sat next to him, his jaw tight and his shoulders rigid. He leaned forward, his head lowered and his fingers twined together. Nick could imagine what was going through Zane's mind. Nick had never had to leave someone he cared for behind, not until now. He understood what the heartbreak felt like.

Ty finally managed to extricate himself from Kelly's hug, and he and planted himself on the floor at Zane's feet, sitting with his seabag behind him as a backrest.

"What happened to your neck?" Ty asked Kelly, pointing to the fingerprints still left under Kelly's chin.

"Nick got carried away during rough sex," Kelly answered, deadpan. Nick muffled a laugh and glanced at Kelly, who winked in return.

Ty rolled his eyes. "Whatever. What time are we expecting Johns and Digger?"

"I'll check the arrivals again," Kelly told them, patting Nick on the shoulder before he walked off, moving slowly and holding his hand to his side. He had grown increasingly restless now that he was on the mend, wanting to push himself more and more.

Nick watched him go, filled with anger and regret that they were here at all and not back in Colorado on Kelly's deck, looking at the stars. That wasn't the only regret on his mind, though. He didn't like having secrets, and though he and Kelly had decided it was best to let this one stay quiet until they returned home and figured things out themselves, it wasn't the only secret Nick was harboring right now.

"What's going on, Irish?" Ty asked as soon as Kelly was out of earshot.

Nick shook his head.

"You look guilty. What have you done?"

Nick glanced at Zane, then back at Ty with a nod. There was no point in trying to hide it once Ty had called him on it. The airport bustled around them, but Nick barely took notice of any of it. He took a deep breath, steeling himself. "I really fucked up this time."

"I'm going to go get some . . . coffee," Zane said as he made to stand.

Nick waved a hand. He sat forward, rubbing his eyes. "It's okay, Garrett. Stay."

"What happened?" Ty asked.

Nick checked to make certain Kelly wasn't on his way back before he took a deep breath. "At the hospital in New Orleans, the day they were releasing the Doc," he said, beginning to tremble as he thought about what Kelly's reaction would be to his admission. "I was getting coffee as we waited for the papers. I saw two sailors at the front desk, getting information."

"Sailors?" Ty asked. "They were there for Doc?"

Nick shrugged. "I don't know. I thought they were. I went back upstairs, found his doctor, and . . ." Nick pushed at the back of his teeth with his tongue, trying to work up the nerve to finish. "I bribed him to say Kelly was no longer fit for service."

Ty sat up straighter, eyes wide. "You what?"

Nick rubbed at his chin, lowering his head.

"Jesus Christ, Nick," Ty whispered he glanced over his shoulder. "Does he know?"

Nick shook his head.

"He can barely walk; there's no way he'd have been called back, regardless," Zane pointed out. "Right?"

"I have to tell him," Nick said.

Ty put his hand on Nick's knee to draw his attention back. "You can't do that, man."

"You didn't see the way he reacted when they came for me and not him. I can't leave him behind thinking he wasn't good enough to come with us."

"That is your guilt talking and making you sound like an idiot," Ty hissed. "He's not physically able to go back. We know that. *He* knows that. He's not stupid. No matter what you did, Doc wouldn't be coming with us. Nothing you can tell him is going to make him feel better about that."

Nick closed his eyes. Damn Ty and his unscrupulous ability to make sense out of lying. When he glanced up again, he saw Kelly working his way across the crowded terminal with Owen in tow.

Ty tapped Nick's knee. "Do you really want him left behind knowing you did this? It can wait until we get back."

"Just stop talking, Beaumont," Nick grunted. "You're like the Bermuda Triangle of morals."

Zane snorted and covered it with a cough.

"Fine, be that way," Ty said. "Go be a goddamn white knight."

"Will he even be angry at all?" Zane asked quietly. "Is Kelly capable of being angry?"

Nick was silent, watching Kelly. He really only had two options. He could man the fuck up and tell Kelly what he'd done, risking his anger here at the eleventh hour. Or he could keep it to himself, working on the logic that Kelly legitimately wouldn't have been recalled anyway. Nick's actions probably had nothing to do with it. But he'd go off to war with the nagging feeling that he was a coward and a horrible friend.

He pushed to his feet before he could talk himself out of it, striding to meet Kelly and Owen as they approached the lounge area. Owen greeted him with a sedate hug. Nick took Kelly's arm and held on as Owen headed for Ty and Zane.

"You okay?" Kelly asked when Nick didn't let go of him.

"I have something I need to tell you."

Kelly glanced at the others and Nick did the same. Owen shook Zane's hand before settling onto the floor beside Ty. Nick found it harder to breathe, but he took Kelly by both shoulders and turned him to face him to make him focus.

"Just be quiet until I finish saying this."

"If this is your way of professing your undying love for me, you need some work on your technique," Kelly drawled.

"I'm the reason you didn't get recalled with us," Nick said in a quiet rush.

Kelly's smile fell and he straightened. "What?"

Nick told him what he'd done in New Orleans, and why he'd done it. "I saw a chance to keep one of us from going back over there, and I took it. I was trying to . . . save you."

Kelly gaped, finally tearing his eyes away from Nick to glance at the others, who were now watching them. He took a step back, jerking out of Nick's grasp.

"Kels, I—"

"How the hell could you do this?" Kelly shouted. He shoved at Nick's shoulder and almost immediately grabbed for his chest, hunching with the pain he'd obviously forgotten would come.

Nick reached to steady him. Kelly swatted at his hand again but Nick gripped his elbow hard and held on, refusing to be pushed away. "I'm sorry," he said, repeating it again and again as Kelly tried to shove him away.

A hand landed on Nick's shoulder, and Owen and Ty were there with them, pulling them apart. Ty gripped Nick's elbows, restraining him. Owen held Kelly's waist to keep him upright, thinking he'd overworked himself and was about to collapse. But Kelly growled and lashed out, catching Nick's chin with his fist before Owen could pull him away.

Nick and Ty both tumbled to the ground.

"Jesus Christ," Ty grunted. He released Nick immediately, giving him the chance to defend himself. Nick didn't move, though.

Kelly stood with his hands on his knees, breathing hard and hanging his head. Owen hovered beside him, a hand on Kelly's back, looking supremely confused.

"What the fuck is going on?" Digger shouted. He stood a few feet away, his seabag on his shoulder.

"Jesus Christ, that really hurt," Kelly gasped. He straightened carefully, holding his chest. "I feel better now."

Digger dropped his bag and helped Ty and Nick to their feet.

"Did that hurt?" Kelly asked Nick.

Nick rubbed his jaw, nodding. "Little bit, yeah."

"Good," Kelly huffed.

He grabbed for Nick's shoulder, catching the material of his shirt and pulling him closer with it. Relief washed through Nick as Kelly hugged him. He rested his chin on Kelly's shoulder and held him tight.

"You did it out of love," Kelly whispered. He patted Nick's shoulder. "And I'd still be stuck here no matter what you did, so . . . you did it out of love. It's okay."

"What the hell happened?" Digger asked again. "And what happened to Doc's neck?"

Kelly snorted in Nick's ear and they both began to laugh.

"You two have spent too much time in Doc's weed," Owen said, walking away now that the drama had passed. The others trailed after him, leaving Nick and Kelly to their embrace.

They sat in a sedate group as the minutes ticked down. Their flight to Jacksonville, North Carolina, was leaving soon, and the last hours felt too heavy to fill with anything meaningful. Nothing would be special enough, so they spent the time telling stories and laughing.

Kelly still hadn't quite come to terms with the fact that he wouldn't be going with them. What the hell was he supposed to do? He kept glancing at Nick. He couldn't even be upset by what Nick had told him. He knew Nick always acted on an almost desperate instinct to protect the people he loved.

Kelly had been joking when he'd guessed Nick was about to profess his undying love, but he hadn't been too far off the mark. Nick's technique was pretty damn good, if not subtle as hell.

They were listening to the story of how Ty had pulled a Rhett Butler on Zane in the middle of the Baltimore FBI field office when they heard the boarding announcement for the flight that would take the boys away.

Kelly's heart jumped into his throat.

Everyone was silent and stoic as they gathered their seabags and walked as a group toward the nearby gate. They gathered at the boarding lanes, trying to figure out how to say good-bye, trying to decide which gestures would last for a lifetime of memories if someone didn't come home.

Ty wrapped Zane up in a hug, his murmured words too low to overhear. They stood that way, grasping each other for dear life.

Kelly took Owen's hand and shook it, pulling him into a hug. "Be safe, bud," he whispered.

"You know what to do, right?" Owen asked.

Kelly nodded and released him. Both Nick and Owen had put Kelly in charge of their affairs. Nick because he had no one else he trusted, and Owen because his parents didn't have the security clearance.

Owen backed away and let Digger move in for a hug. He bypassed the handshake entirely and picked Kelly up, squeezing him to the point that it hurt. Kelly laughed breathlessly and patted his back until Digger set him down again. Digger turned away without a word, sniffing audibly.

Kelly forced himself to meet Nick's eyes. Nick moved close and hugged him gently, pressing their cheeks together, his warm hands splayed against Kelly's back. "I don't have the words," he whispered.

"You don't need them," Kelly said shakily. "Just watch your damn six out there."

Nick nodded jerkily and moved away, his head down and his shoulders slumped. Kelly fought back tears as he looked at the three of them. His boys.

Ty grabbed Kelly's face and kissed his forehead, patting his cheek. "Be good," he said gruffly before moving away. He joined the others, all of them turning to face Kelly and Zane. They went to attention without a word, standing shoulder to shoulder. Then each of them gave a sharp salute.

Kelly finally lost control and let the tears track down his face without wiping them away. He straightened and returned their salute, holding it until the four remaining members of Force Recon Team Sidewinder turned away and headed for the gangway, walking once again into the fray.

Not one of them looked back.

"Oh God," Zane whispered.

"They'll be okay," Kelly said shakily.

Zane sniffed and nodded. "Yeah. It's us I'm worried about."

Kelly didn't tear his eyes away from the gangway until the last man was out of sight. Then he turned to Zane. "Nick O'Flaherty doesn't make a promise he doesn't intend to die trying to keep."

"He made me a promise," Zane said.

Kelly nodded, swallowing hard. "Me too."

# BAIT & SWITCH

## A SIDEWINDER STORY

ABIGAIL ROUX

Zane was on his way up the stairs when the doorbell rang. He debated not answering it, but ultimately he headed back down, grumbling. It was Sunday, his only day off, and he didn't want to deal with any shit today.

He peered through the peephole, and his heart stuttered when he saw the Marine on the stoop. He was wearing a green and khaki service uniform, a barracks cover on his head. A seabag was slung over his shoulder, and he stood straight and tall as he looked out on the street, his back to the door.

Zane fumbled with the lock, his fingers suddenly unable to keep up with his racing heart. Was it news? Was it good or bad news? Why the hell would a Marine be standing on his stoop if it wasn't news?

He swung the door open, feeling stupid and clumsy as the man turned to face him.

"O'Flaherty?"

Nick gave him a wan smile and held up his hand. "No one's hurt."

Zane glared at him. He wasn't sure whether to believe him or not. And he wasn't sure whether to hug him or hit him.

Nick laughed at Zane's expression, the sound flat and tired. "Nothing's wrong, I promise."

Zane looked him up and down, inspecting him for injuries that would have sent him home. None were visible. "Why are you here? *How* are you here?"

"Forty-eight-hour special liberty."

Zane frowned harder. He realized he was still gripping the door, and his knuckles hurt. He let go and shook his hand. "Special liberty?" he asked carefully.

"I have a cold," Nick answered, deadpan. He waited a beat. "Can I come in?"

Zane started, nodding as he stepped out of the way. "Yeah. Shit. Sorry, I just . . ."

"Panicked, I know. I'm sorry, I didn't have anywhere to change out of the uniform," Nick said as he stepped inside. He set his seabag down by the door, the same spot Ty always dropped his gym bag when he was tired after a long day.

Zane stared at it for a moment, letting the pain settle in his chest before he tried to take another breath. He finally tore his eyes away and tried to smile at Nick. Nick was watching him. He seemed exhausted, but his frown was sympathetic. He had to sense Zane's disappointment that he wasn't Ty.

"You look good," Zane managed to say with a wave of his hand at Nick.

Nick smirked. "I know. Marines always look good." He reached into his back pocket and pulled out a leather billfold that appeared to hold his orders, then pulled a creased and battered envelope from the billfold and handed it to Zane.

Zane stared at it, licking his lips and steeling himself before he reached for it. It was warm against his fingers, and the simple scrawl of his name was familiar. It was from Ty, but it had the appearance of a letter that had seen many nights in someone's pocket. Zane knew a lot of soldiers, sailors, and Marines left a letter with a buddy in case they didn't make it home. If Nick had been carrying this letter around every day for that reason, Zane didn't want to read it. "This isn't . . ."

"He knew I was coming home," Nick answered, voice gentle. "He wrote it before I left."

Zane released the breath he'd been holding in a rush. He turned the letter over, fingers shaking, desperate to rip it open and read the first communication he'd received from Ty in months.

Nick cleared his throat. "Garrett. I know my way around if you want to take that upstairs and read it. You can write him a response and I'll carry it back with me."

Zane blinked at him, fighting to breathe. "You only have forty-eight hours. You shouldn't waste them."

Nick raised both eyebrows and shook his head. "I'm not."

Zane stared at him for another breathless second, then lunged and wrapped Nick up in a hug. Nick began to laugh, patting him on the back awkwardly. "Go on," he finally urged. "I'm going to steal some of Ty's Cubans while you do that."

"Deal." Zane backed away and then turned to head up the stairs, the letter pressed to his hip so his fingers wouldn't tremble as he held it. He heard Nick in the kitchen, probably retrieving the portable safe Ty kept hidden below the kitchen sink where he stowed his Cuban cigars. Zane didn't even care that Nick knew it was there. He went to his bedroom and sat on the end of the bed, staring down at the letter from Ty.

He almost didn't want to open it. There was every possibility it might be the last thing he heard from Ty, and though he tried not to think that way, he was only human. The notion kept creeping in. What if this was it? What if this was the last thing they managed to say to each other? How could it ever be enough?

He forced himself to tear into the envelope before he could make himself sick.

*Zane,*

*I'm okay. We're all okay. I miss you like nothing I've ever experienced, and I wanted you to know that. I can't say more. Please don't ask Nick details. Just know we're doing our damnedest to get home.*

It was signed formally, with the words Captain B. Tyler Grady scrawled across the bottom.

"Captain," Zane murmured. He smiled even as his composure threatened. There was almost nothing to go on, but it was from Ty and that was all that mattered. Beneath the signature were eight numbers that seemed to be random. Zane wondered first if they were perhaps a processing code, but they were in Ty's handwriting.

After staring for a few more seconds, he realized what it was. A simple cipher. Ty had sent him an encoded message. He grabbed a pad of paper from the bedside table and began writing down the letters needed to replace the numbers, and it didn't take long to decipher what the message said: "I love you."

Zane began to laugh. Ty had sent him a puzzle to play with.

It took him long minutes to write his response. He kept it just as short, just as succinct, knowing these letters were being read. He included his own cipher in return, with the message, "Aye aye, Captain," just to throw Ty off.

He didn't seal it, knowing it wouldn't matter, and then thumped back down the stairs. Nick was nowhere to be found, though. The living room was silent, and nothing was out of place. Zane called his name, cocking his head to listen.

The distant reply came from outside. Zane ambled out to the front stoop, but again he found no one there. "Nick?"

"Up here," Nick called.

Zane craned his head, peering two stories up to the top floor balcony where Nick stood, leaning over and looking at him.

"How the fuck did you get past me?" Zane asked, chuckling at the memory of Nick and Kelly scaling a balcony in New Orleans.

"I have skills," Nick said, his voice just low enough to travel down. He waved the cigar held between two long fingers. "Come share this thing with me."

He disappeared over the railing, and Zane headed back inside to join him. He climbed past the bedrooms on the second floor and into the large attic room, where the door to the balcony was propped open and the curtains were flowing in a light breeze. He stood in the doorway, watching Nick for a moment. Nick was reclining in a rusty old lawn chair, his feet propped on the railing. He'd changed into jeans and a black T-shirt, and he was barefoot.

He held up the Cuban for Zane to take, and Zane moved to sit in the chair beside him, putting the cigar in his mouth. He studied Nick for several more seconds.

Zane had never paid a lot of attention to Nick, other than briefly deciding he was going to try to like him instead of hit him. He didn't know him well, even though he was so much like Ty on the surface. He didn't know his moods, and he couldn't read him. But even Zane could see that Nick wasn't the same person he'd been in New Orleans.

"Got a response?" Nick asked when he finally turned to Zane and smiled.

Zane handed him the envelope. "Are you okay?" he asked impulsively.

Nick glanced up from folding the letter, his eyebrows jumping. "Why?"

"Well, I mean . . . you're here. You're not in Boston. I know I wasn't the top person on your list to see, so . . . are you okay?"

Nick smiled, looking away from Zane to peer out over the city stretching beyond the balcony. Zane had sat up here with Ty many times. It was where Ty liked to come to think, to ponder their cases, to decompress after a stressful day. Nick had obviously been up here enough to know that if he hadn't propped the door open, he would have gotten locked out.

"I'm not okay," he finally said, his voice so soft and hoarse that Zane had to lean closer to hear.

Zane held his breath, waiting for Nick to elaborate. Nick remained silent, though.

"O'Flaherty," Zane finally whispered.

Nick lowered his head, licking his lips. "I never thanked you for what you did."

"What?"

"Ty is my best friend," Nick said. "He's been the most constant thing I've had in my life. I know if you had forced him to choose between us, he would have chosen you. And he should have," Nick added quickly with a glance at Zane. "Thank you for not making him choose."

Zane had to take a few seconds to gather his thoughts as Nick met his gaze with striking green eyes. He finally found his voice. "I'm glad I didn't. It would have killed him."

They sat in silence, staring at each other for several more moments. Zane didn't feel awkward about it, and the moment didn't strike him as especially heavy or fraught. Nick had a way of making him feel at ease despite their shaky start, and Zane had to wonder if that was why he and Ty had remained so close for so long. Nick was the rock to Ty's hurricane. He was impervious to Ty's moods. It was like his superpower.

Nick plucked the cigar from Zane's fingers and took a long drag. When he spoke again, smoke accompanied his words. "Doc's flying in to meet up with me. He should be here soon. We'll probably get some dinner. You're welcome to come."

"I'd like that. Thank you."

Nick smiled and took another drag.

Zane laughed at the devious look in Nick's eyes. "Oh my God. Ty told you to take me out to dinner, didn't he?"

"That's classified," Nick drawled. He tilted his head back and blew a smoke ring toward the sunset.

"Great," Zane grumbled. His eyes followed the ring as it wavered off on the breeze. He'd have to get Ty to teach him how to do that when he returned. "Now I'm a charity case."

"Aren't we all, Garrett?"

Zane nodded, smiling wryly. He propped his feet up on the railing. "I've always been a little jealous of you and Ty," he admitted.

Nick glanced at him.

"I never had a friend like that. Someone I knew would be there no matter what. I can't imagine what that's like."

Nick pursed his lips and gave a slow nod. "Garrett, you have at least one friend like that now."

Zane found his throat tightening at the sentiment. He didn't fool himself into thinking Nick was offering any kind of loyalty that wasn't attached to Ty, but it was more than he could remember having in years. "Thank you."

Nick began to smile, and his words took on a sly hint. "So, dinner. You like Italian?"

Zane burst out laughing. "I know a place nearby."

They were both still snickering when they heard a car door shut on the street below. "I see your smoke rings!" Kelly called from below. "I hear your evil cackling."

Nick sat up and peered over the railing, then pushed out of his seat and left Zane sitting there without another word. He didn't make a sound going down the stairs. Zane waved to Kelly, who had a bag slung over his shoulder and was craning his neck to peer up at him.

"Where'd Irish go?"

Before Zane could answer, Nick burst out the front door and hopped the three steps to the sidewalk. He body-slammed Kelly hard and picked him up. Kelly made a sound like a bird being hit by a car, but then he wrapped his arms and legs around Nick and held on as he was hugged.

Zane laughed even as a melancholy ache settled in his chest. He was glad to see the two friends reunited, but he couldn't help but wish that was him and Ty down there.

"Not too long now," he whispered to himself. "Keep it together, Garrett."

Nick had been sent halfway across the world under the guise of a forty-eight-hour mental health break, but his true purpose had been to deliver a single, five-word message to the Office of Naval Intelligence in Suitland, Maryland. He'd flown twelve hours in a jump seat, delivered his message, then diverted to Baltimore to drop in on Zane. Ty hadn't sent him there as Zane had suspected, but Nick hadn't let Zane know that.

He'd been able to get word to Kelly, who'd flown in to meet up with him. Nick had been nearly sick with nerves as he waited for Kelly to arrive, but the moment he'd seen him standing on the sidewalk in front of Ty's row house, the moment he'd heard his lighthearted voice, any trace of apprehension abandoned him and all he wanted was to hug Kelly until his head popped off.

They took Zane to dinner, keeping conversation light, trying not to let anything slip. Kelly knew not to ask questions, and Zane seemed to catch on quickly that even asking how the weather had been was too far.

Dinner was good. Zane's waiter friend, Ryan, was just as hot as Ty complained about. Nick and Kelly were able to keep their hands and eyes off each other for hours as they sat and talked with Zane. In the end, Kelly and Zane arranged to keep in contact better, offering each other some support while Sidewinder was gone.

Zane was clearly heartsick, but he didn't seem lonely. When they parted at the end of the night, he didn't linger or ask them to stick around, though he did offer to let them stay with him. They declined for . . . obvious reasons. But Nick was relieved to see that Zane seemed to be doing okay on his own.

Nick couldn't tell Zane and Kelly that they weren't the only ones who were alone a lot of the time. He couldn't tell them that the team had been split up, promoted and seeded into smaller groups. Given the real reason they'd been recalled—black ops missions on which MARSOC couldn't afford to use known operators—Nick and Digger were now master sergeants, each leading a recon squadron of twelve men. Ty was a captain who commanded four separate squadrons, Nick's and Digger's included. Owen had been filtered into Naval Intelligence, and they only heard from him when they gathered in the dark to do their real jobs.

None of that mattered tonight, though. None of that mattered for the next two days. Nick wrapped his arm around Kelly's waist and pulled him closer as they walked down the hallway to their hotel room. They glanced at each other, both grinning. Neither of them said a word.

Nick slid the room key home and shoved the door open, then reached out to take Kelly's hand and tug him inside. They barely got their bags into the room. They were kissing even before the door latched.

Kelly grasped at Nick's shirt, sliding his hands around to dig into Nick's shoulders. Nick moved in on him, his hands on Kelly's cheeks, shoving him against the wall with little regard for how rough he was being. They both grunted when Kelly hit, but it didn't slow them down. Nick kissed him hungrily, gripping Kelly's hair. Kelly moaned when Nick's fingers tightened and tugged, and the sound was like a dinner bell ringing.

Nick bit Kelly's lip, gasping as their bodies pressed together. "I thought about this so goddamn many times."

Kelly nodded. "Every night. Every fucking night I thought about you."

Nick closed his eyes, running the tip of his nose from Kelly's chin to his cheek, breathing him in. Kelly jutted his chin out and brushed his lips against Nick's. Nick could feel him grinning, could feel the eagerness in his labored breaths. They both knew what was coming. There was no holding it off this time, and there was no point in wasting what precious little time they had in trying to deny what they both wanted.

Nick kissed him, rocking into him. Then he trailed kisses down his chin to his neck and nipped at him, seeking the sounds he remembered Kelly making. He wasn't disappointed. Kelly moaned, vibrating Nick's lips as he sucked on Kelly's neck. Nick grabbed his thighs and picked him up, sliding him up the wall and using his body to keep him there.

Kelly wrapped his legs around Nick's waist to help him. "Fuck me, Nick."

Nick's fingers tightened in his hair and he bit down harder on his neck, dragging his teeth over the skin. He wanted nothing more than to do just that, and now that Kelly wasn't injured, Nick didn't have to worry about hurting him. Much.

"Next time," Nick promised, despite his desire to say "Aye aye" and toss Kelly to the floor.

Kelly grunted. "Now."

Nick laughed and pushed his face against Kelly's neck. "We both need to get off at least once before I get at you, or I'll tear you apart."

"No, you won't! I've been practicing!" Kelly began popping the buttons on Nick's shirt, fingers fluttering against Nick's skin as they moved.

Nick's breath caught. His knees went weak, and he let Kelly slide back down the wall to his feet. He placed both hands on either side of Kelly's head and pushed away so he could meet Kelly's eyes. "Practicing?"

Kelly hummed, biting his lip against a grin.

"How've you been doing that, exactly?" The hoarse rumble in his voice could have been misconstrued as threatening, but Kelly just grinned wider. He knew Nick too well to misconstrue anything he did.

"Jesus, I love it when you do that," Kelly muttered, his changeable eyes boldly meeting Nick's. He undid the button of Nick's jeans with nimble fingers.

"Do what?" Nick asked, his voice gone even rougher. He looked down at Kelly's hands. Kelly pressed his forehead to Nick's, both of them watching as he shoved Nick's jeans down his hips.

"I had a lot of nights alone," Kelly said. Nick raised his head, and their noses brushed. Kelly's breath was warm against his lips. "I called your name every damn time."

"Kels," Nick whispered.

"Try me, babe. I can take it."

Nick's chest tightened, making his breath stutter. His fingers curled against the wall. Kelly's palms slid along his hips, just under the band of his boxers. Then Kelly put his head against the wall and peered up at Nick, smirking as he wrapped his fingers around Nick's cock.

"Just how much self-control do you have left after three months in the desert?"

Nick gripped the back of Kelly's neck and forced him flat against the wall. "Not enough," he snarled before they shared a violent kiss. His other hand tugged haphazardly at Kelly's clothing.

"Fuck me, Nick."

"Shut up, Kels. Just stop talking."

Kelly laughed. "I can't shut up, I talk when I'm nervous!"

Nick snorted and shoved away from the wall. He met Kelly's eyes, running his knuckles down his cheek. Months of thoughts swirled in his head, months of thinking that he could love Kelly, that they could really work. He wanted to tell Kelly just that, but now wasn't the time. He wasn't the type of man who hid his emotions, though, so he knew Kelly was seeing hints of it in his eyes.

"Babe," Kelly murmured.

When they kissed again, neither of them closed their eyes.

Kelly's fingers were gentle against Nick's skin. Nick cupped his face and kissed him again, humming as Kelly's body relaxed further. Nick didn't want him nervous, not for any reason.

"Does this feel right?" he asked, his lips moving against the corner of Kelly's mouth.

Kelly sighed shakily, then took a deep breath. "Yes," he whispered. "It feels like home."

Nick pushed his nose against Kelly's, kissing him gently as warmth spread through his entire body.

"*You* feel like home," Kelly said as he wrapped his arms around Nick's neck.

Nick couldn't find his breath, and everything else seemed to fade away except for the feeling of Kelly in his arms. He slowed everything down, kissing Kelly languidly. They had to separate for air, and Nick pushed away from the wall. They met each other's eyes, not saying anything, not feeling the need to.

Kelly reached to lift Nick's T-shirt up, but Nick took his hand instead.

Kelly's eyes narrowed. "What?"

Nick tried to verbalize what he was feeling, but he didn't even know what it was. It was so much more than just sex. "Kels," he finally managed.

"No, don't do that! We only have two nights and we're supposed to be having hot monkey sex! You can't back out on me now!"

Nick burst out laughing, covering his face with one hand. "'You feel like home'! You can't have hot monkey sex after that!"

"Yes you can!" Kelly insisted. He grabbed the hem of Nick's shirt and yanked it up, shoving it up over his head and then tossing it to the floor. He shoved Nick toward the bed. "I'll show you."

Nick stumbled backward, barely able to keep his balance with his jeans riding low around his thighs. "Kelly!"

Kelly shoved him again. "Don't fight it, Irish, come have your way with me."

Nick licked his lips and grumbled, but Kelly shoved him one last time and he wound up on his back on the mattress. Kelly yanked his shirt off as he headed for the door and the bags they'd dropped. He was out of sight for a moment, then he returned, naked, with both hands full. He held up a bottle of lubricant in one, and a red flipcam in the other.

"Is that a video camera?" Nick asked, his voice cracking.

Kelly stuck his tongue out, biting it as he nodded.

"You're crazy," Nick drawled, unable to keep the affection out of his voice.

Kelly set both his prizes on the bed and untied Nick's shoes, pulling each one off and dropping it with a heavy thunk to the floor. Then he pulled Nick's jeans off, followed by his boxers, and climbed onto the bed to straddle Nick.

"Please tell me you haven't been practicing with someone like this?" Nick said with a strained laugh.

Kelly put both hands on Nick's chest and leaned over him. "Maybe I'll show you later how I've been spending my nights."

Nick grunted and Kelly shifted, moving against Nick's hard cock. Their eyes met, and they both grinned.

"Don't hold back, Irish," Kelly taunted.

Nick licked his lips, his eyes raking down Kelly's body. He sat up, kissing at the scar on Kelly's chest and up his throat to his jaw. Kelly shifted around in his lap, rubbing his ass against Nick's cock. Nick held him tighter and kicked his leg out to the side, using the leverage to flip them both and pin Kelly beneath him. They stretched out sideways on the king-sized bed. Kelly arched his back and squeezed his legs against Nick's hips.

"Jesus Christ, Kelly."

Kelly laughed and grabbed Nick's face. "No. Whose name do you say?"

"Yours," Nick growled.

Kelly bit Nick's lip as they kissed, not letting go even when Nick pulled back. Nick took hold of his hips and yanked him toward the edge of the bed, scooting back and pulling Kelly with him. When his feet hit the floor, he stood and grabbed Kelly's legs to flip him over to his stomach. Kelly flailed and grabbed at the bedcovers, but he couldn't right himself before Nick had him pinned again.

He leaned over him, sliding his hand under Kelly and up his chest to pull their bodies together, his cock hard against Kelly's ass. Kelly tilted his head to offer up his neck, and Nick bit down, dragging one hand to grip Kelly's hip. Nick could feel Kelly's heart hammering against his palm, beating in frantic time with his own.

"Is this how you want it?" Kelly asked. He moved his ass against Nick's cock, making them both moan.

Nick put his lips to Kelly's ear, holding him tighter. "I want you every fucking way I can get you."

Kelly stretched his lean body out to reach for the bottle of lubricant. Nick ran his hand over Kelly's spine, letting his cock slide against his ass. Good God, he was absolutely sinuous. Nick couldn't wait to be inside him, to make him writhe.

Kelly handed the lubricant back to him. Nick took the bottle, barely able to stay under control. "We don't have condoms?"

"Don't need them." Kelly's voice was muffled as he rested on his elbows and hung his head.

Nick rubbed his palm over Kelly's ass, bending over to kiss his shoulder. "Okay," he whispered, despite a jolt of nerves, then snapped the bottle open. He straightened back up, stroking himself and watching the rapid rise and fall of Kelly's breathing. "Hand me that fucking video camera."

Kelly made a whimpering sound and reached for it, snagging it by the attached string. He turned it on and handed it to Nick. Nick hit record and bent over Kelly to speak against his ear. "I better not see this shit on the internet."

Kelly pushed up and made an exasperated sound. "Just hurry up and get in there!"

Nick gripped him by his shoulder, laughing. He stroked himself, covering his cock liberally in lube. "Last chance."

Kelly shivered in Nick's arms and turned his head, seeking Nick's lips with his own. As they kissed, Nick reached between them, pressing one slick finger against Kelly's asshole. Kelly groaned wantonly and rested his forehead on the bed, giving Nick the perfect opening to kiss along his shoulder and neck—kisses Kelly leaned into, and their lips meeting again. Nick slid his tongue into Kelly's mouth as he slid his finger inside him. It was an easy entry, a gasp and a tightening of muscles Kelly's only reaction.

"You *have* been practicing," Nick growled.

"Try me."

Nick's heart was pounding, making it hard to breathe, making it hard to even think. Kelly's body was warm and hard against his. He'd imagined this so many times over the last few months. He'd fucking craved it.

He worked a second finger inside, moving slowly, twisting, turning the video camera to record it. Kelly arched his body and rewarded him with another deep moan.

"Kels," Nick gritted out.

"Fuck me, Nick, come on."

Nick took himself in hand and pushed the head of his cock against Kelly's ass, pressing forward. Kelly shoved his knee against Nick's to widen his stance. He was hanging his head and panting, and Nick hadn't even pushed inside him yet.

Nick put a hand in the center of his back and said, "Breathe out, babe."

Kelly did, and Nick worked the head of his cock inside him, watching and barely remembering to point the camera toward the action.

"Jesus fucking Christ, Kels," Nick gasped. He closed his eyes and fought with every ounce of willpower he possessed not to shove in deeper. "I've never been inside someone without a condom."

"First for both of us then," Kelly said, his voice strained. He raised his head, pushing up on his hands. "Goddamn."

Nick ran his hand down Kelly's spine. "Okay?"

Kelly's answer came out as a hiss. "Fuck yes."

He hung his head again, pushing his hips back carefully. Nick didn't move, letting Kelly guide the entry. Kelly groaned louder, going still, and Nick began to rotate his hips, working himself inside. He'd never felt anything like it.

"Yeah, babe," Kelly grunted, grabbing at Nick's hip, digging his fingers in and pulling Nick closer. Nick sank further in and gasped, gripping Kelly hard.

"Fuck, Kelly, this isn't going to last long if you don't fucking control yourself."

"You fucking control it," Kelly grunted. He shoved back again and they both shouted as Nick sank deep.

Nick fumbled with the video camera and raised it to capture himself pulling his cock slowly out and then rocking back in.

"Fuck!" Kelly cried. He grabbed at the covers, his fingers twisting in them.

Nick seated himself, shoving deep, then leaned over and placed his hand on top of Kelly's, twining their fingers.

"Wreck me, babe," Kelly pleaded.

"Fuck," Nick gritted out. He dropped the camera and grabbed Kelly's hip instead, pulling out and carefully thrusting back in. It took him longer than usual to find a good rhythm, but goddamn Kelly was so fucking tight he had to go slow. He *wanted* to go slow. He rested his head against Kelly's shoulder and fucked him, pushing in deep and pulling out until Kelly pleaded. Rolled his hips and tugged at Kelly until both their toes curled.

Kelly's moans grew louder, his body writhing, his ass so tight Nick thought he might come every time Kelly moved. Kelly finally pushed onto his hands and knees, gasping for breath. He reached out, his hand fumbling for the video camera. He shoved it under him, pointing it so they'd be able to watch from below as Nick fucked him.

Nick buried himself deep and began to laugh. "You're dirty, Kels."

"That's like Satan calling me a bad boy."

Nick laughed harder and bent over him, rocking into him. Kelly shouted, caught by the new angle.

"Oh Jesus, hello prostate," he gasped.

Nick gripped his hip hard and hit that angle again. Over and over, until Kelly was barely able to prop himself up anymore. Nick paused just long enough to add more lube to the mix, then sped his rhythm, still aiming for Kelly's prostate. Their bodies pounded together, the slapping of their skin masked only by Kelly's shouts for more.

"Fuck, Nick, I'm gonna come," Kelly managed after several minutes.

"Are you fucking kidding me?" Nick gasped. "You're seriously one of those that can come without being jacked?"

"Keep going."

"God, I love you," Nick said as Kelly's muscles began to tighten and spasm. "If you come, I'm going to."

Kelly threw his head back. "You'll come inside me?"

"Or on you, wherever the fuck you want."

Kelly moaned. "Shoot it off inside me, Lucky. Fill me up."

The bed protested Nick's thrusts, but Kelly cried out for more. Nick watched his cock disappearing into Kelly's ass, his fingers digging into the muscles. The red camera was still sitting on the bed, watching everything, recording it from below. Kelly would probably jack off to this video for weeks. Nick winked at the camera.

Kelly cried out, throwing his head back.

"Whose name do you say?" Nick demanded.

"Oh God," Kelly whimpered.

Nick pounded into him harder. "Say it, babe, come on. Whose name?"

"Yours!" Kelly shouted.

Nick rammed into him, rotating his hips to massage Kelly's prostate. "I'm sorry, I couldn't hear you. Who?"

"Fucking hell, Nick! I'm going to come!"

"You'll come when I tell you to. You'll come when you start screaming my fucking name."

Nick grabbed Kelly's shoulder to hold him still, slowing his thrusts so he could feel Kelly's orgasm when it came. Kelly fought against being held, but he had nowhere to go. His fingers clutched at the covers. His hips moved, desperately trying to force Nick's cock to hit his prostate again.

"Nick," he finally pled.

Nick's voice was gruff as he tried to hold off on his own orgasm. "You want it?"

"Yeah, babe. Please, please."

"You're so fucking good at begging."

"I want it, baby, come on! I want it!"

"Let me hear you come," Nick growled. He shoved in deep and Kelly cried out incoherently. Nick kept hitting that spot, over and over, his thrusts hard and fast, never pulling out, keeping the pressure on Kelly's prostate.

"Nick!" Kelly's back arched like a cat. His entire body spasmed. The muscles around Nick's cock squeezed, making it almost impossible for him to move. He kept going though, fucking Kelly through his orgasm as he reached under him to finally take Kelly's cock in his hand. He hadn't even fucking touched Kelly's cock, not once, but Kelly's cum was spurting against the bed. He really was coming just from taking it up the ass. God, he was fun to fuck! Nick jacked him off, causing Kelly to shout again. "Nick!"

Nick growled. "Get it all out, babe."

Kelly finally lost the ability to keep himself up, though he had the wherewithal to grab the camera before he collapsed, and he pointed it over his shoulder so it would record Nick, still buried deep inside him, still fucking him. Nick gave the camera a cheeky nod.

He readjusted to the new position, putting both hands on Kelly's ass cheeks and pushing them apart so he could see his cock sliding in and out. It was almost like doing push-ups, except far more fun.

"Come on, Nick," Kelly grunted. He stretched out, holding the camera out so it would pan down the expanse of his own sweaty back and capture Nick's thick cock shoving into his ass. "I know you've got a load for me."

"I do," Nick growled.

"It's got to be a big one, babe. Let me have it."

Nick bent over, his thrusts losing their rhythm. Kelly's moans and gasps grew louder, spurring him on until he couldn't hold back any longer—and he didn't want to. He pulled out, pumping his slick cock until cum began to shoot against Kelly's ass, then shoved himself back in, shouting as the friction overwhelmed him. He laid out over Kelly, pulling him tight, gasping his name, rocking his hips as he emptied himself deep inside him.

They were both left slick and breathless. Nick could already feel the cum dripping from Kelly's ass, being pushed back out by the tightening of his muscles around Nick's cock.

After several long moments of merely trying to breathe, Nick rolled his hips, and they both moaned. Kelly shifted beneath him.

"Did you just shoot off inside me?"

Nick chuckled. "Yeah. Yeah, I did."

"God, that's so fucking hot."

Nick kissed the back of his shoulder and pushed up. "I'm pulling out of you now. You ready?"

Kelly nodded, but when Nick started to move, Kelly gasped and his muscles tightened. "Jesus Christ, are you still fucking hard in there?"

Nick couldn't help but laugh again. He reached for Kelly's chin, turning his head to the side to kiss him. He licked at Kelly. "Kiss me."

Kelly did, parting his lips so Nick could slip his tongue inside. He deepened the kiss, making it a slow, languid exploration of Kelly's lips and tongue and teeth to keep Kelly's mind off the fact that he was pulling out.

When he was free, he rolled and flopped at Kelly's side. Their feet hung off the edge of the bed. They stared at each other, neither saying anything, neither moving.

"So," Kelly finally said. "What's your recovery time like?"

Nick rolled to his back and laughed.

"I'm serious. I've never sucked cock either. I want to try that next."

"Oh God."

"No, you say my name when I suck you off, bitch," Kelly drawled as he pulled himself closer and rested his elbow on Nick's chest. He kissed Nick and grinned. "You know what?"

Nick rested his hands under his head, letting Kelly cuddle closer to him. "What?"

"You came inside me." He smiled and bit his lip.

Nick's body flushed even though he'd just exhausted himself. It was the first time he'd ever come inside someone, if he didn't count blowjobs. The thought was hotter than he'd expected. His words were choked. "Yes, I did."

"That makes me so fucking hot just thinking about it," Kelly admitted.

Nick kissed him again, gripping his hair to keep him from moving away. He reached down with the other hand to grab Kelly's ass, his fingers trailing through slick cum.

"Babe," Nick growled.

"I feel it. You filled me up. I knew you had a load for me."

"You're so fucking dirty, I love it."

"You won't even need lube next time."

Nick closed his eyes. "Next time will be pretty damn soon if you keep this up."

Kelly kissed him again, dragging his teeth against Nick's lip. "Next time I'm going to ride you. God, your dick is fun, you know that? And I get to hold the camera too."

Nick slid his sticky hands into Kelly's hair, narrowing his eyes. Kelly's expression turned guarded, like he thought Nick might be irritated by the presence of the recording device now that he wasn't lost in the haze of lust.

Nick grinned. "Good call on the waterproof camera."

Kelly laughed. He bent to kiss Nick, molding to his body as they both lay sideways on the bed. Nick held him close and Kelly settled into the crook of his arm, resting his head on Nick's shoulder.

"I'm glad you're back, even if it is just forty-eight hours."

Nick buried his face in Kelly's hair. "Me too."

"Are you okay, Irish?"

Nick nodded.

"It's me you're talking to," Kelly murmured.

Nick was silent. He finally nodded again. "Yeah, I'm okay."

Kelly held him tighter and turned into him, closing his eyes. "All these years, and you're still a shitty liar."

Nick woke to the disturbing sound of utter silence. The room was still, the expensive hotel's infrastructure buffering the sounds from other rooms. The A/C had shut off. It took several moments for Nick to shake the confusion of finding himself in a soft, cool bed. It took him a few more to realize he was alone.

He stretched his hand out, running his fingers across the indentation in the pillow next to him.

"Kels?" he called out. He held his breath, nerves beginning to build when there was no answer.

He sat up and pushed the sheets away, looking around the hotel room. Pillows and clothing littered the floor. The comforter was gone. One of the bedside lamps had been knocked over. Nick could feel a split in his lip where Kelly had bit him. The chaise in the corner had been used for horrible things. The only thing missing was Kelly.

Nick slid out of bed and dug through his seabag for a clean pair of jeans. He was still zipping them up when he stepped out onto the balcony to find Kelly sitting with his feet propped on the railing, wrapped in the comforter from the bed.

"Hey," Kelly said without looking over at him.

"Thought you'd bailed on me for a minute," Nick told him, smiling. "What are you doing out here?"

Kelly shrugged, too busy chewing on his lip to answer.

Nick squinted out at the harbor, frowning. He couldn't see anything that might be keeping Kelly's attention. He took a step toward him, but something stopped him from moving closer. "You okay?"

"I was wrong," Kelly said almost immediately, like he'd been waiting for a pin to pop a balloon. He gazed up at Nick, his eyes blue and full of sorrow in the morning light. "I can't do this."

The words hit Nick square in the chest, stealing his breath. He realized he was staring, meeting Kelly's eyes as he tried to reconcile such a swift ending to something he'd thought would be . . . permanent. He took a careful step and sat in the nearest chair, nodding and clearing his throat to try to play off his natural reaction. "Okay," he managed.

"I'm sorry," Kelly whispered. He was watching Nick, turned toward him with that stupid blanket around his shoulders.

Nick couldn't look at him, though, not until he was sure the devastation was off his face. He nodded again. "It's okay, Kels. Nothing to apologize for. We knew it might not work, right?"

"I thought I could do it, I really did. But you said it was nothing more than sex." Kelly paused, giving Nick a chance to speak or react. Nick couldn't find his voice. Jesus, why did this hurt so fucking much? Kelly cleared his throat. "It's already more than that, though."

Nick glanced at him sharply, his heart skipping.

Kelly shrugged, giving him a weak smile. "We both know how fast I fall."

"Kelly—"

"I think we're better off if we just stop now," Kelly said quickly. "The thought of this being something . . . frivolous? The thought of you going home and being with someone else? It kind of breaks my heart, bud."

"Someone else," Nick repeated, his voice hoarse.

"We both know how friends with benefits work, Irish, come on."

Nick leaned forward and grabbed Kelly's hand. He swallowed past the nerves and the fear and met Kelly's changeable eyes with a deep breath. "Kels, I can't think of a thing under the sun that makes me happier than you."

Kelly blinked rapidly, his mouth parting in shock.

Nick held his hand tighter. "If it doesn't feel right to you, you say the word and this'll be it. But if you'll give me a chance, just one chance, I swear to you I'll make it worth it."

"A chance at what?"

"To be yours."

Kelly tried several times to speak. He licked dry lips and said, "Nick."

"Do you trust me, Kels?"

"You know I do."

Nick held his breath, waiting for the verdict. Kelly's lips twitched, then he began to grin. He reached out and caught Nick by the back of his neck, pulling him into an urgent kiss. Nick grabbed him by the edges of his blanket, wrapping it around them both as Kelly crawled onto the chaise lounge with him and straddled him.

"Is that a yes?" Nick managed to ask between kisses.

Kelly bit his lip, dragging his teeth across it before nodding. "Don't ask stupid questions."

Nick laughed, holding him closer. "We're really going to try this, aren't we?"

Kelly was grinning against his lips as he nodded. "Does this mean I get to say I love you and you have to say it back?"

Nick chuckled. "Yeah. That's what it means."

Kelly pressed his forehead to Nick's. "I love you, Nick O'Flaherty."

Nick's heart jumped into his throat. He was grinning so widely it hurt his split lip. "I love you. You crazy bastard."

# ALSO BY ABIGAIL ROUX

*The Cut & Run Series:*

#1: Cut & Run (with Madeleine Urban)

#2: Sticks & Stones (with Madeleine Urban)

#3: Fish & Chips (with Madeleine Urban)

#4: Divide & Conquer (with Madeleine Urban)

#5: Armed & Dangerous

#6: Stars & Stripes

#7: Touch & Geaux

*Novels:*

The Gravedigger's Brawl

According to Hoyle

Caught Running (with Madeleine Urban)

Love Ahead (with Madeleine Urban)

The Archer

Warrior's Cross (with Madeleine Urban)

*Novellas:*

A Tale from de Rode

My Brother's Keeper

Seeing Is Believing

Unrequited

# About The Author

Abigail Roux was born and raised in North Carolina. A past volleyball star who specializes in sarcasm and painful historical accuracy, she currently spends her time coaching high school volleyball and investigating the mysteries of single motherhood. Any spare time is spent living and dying with every Atlanta Braves and Carolina Panthers game of the year. Abigail has a daughter, Little Roux, who is the light of her life, a boxer, four rescued cats who play an ongoing live-action variation of *Call of Duty* throughout the house, one evil Ragdoll, a certifiable extended family down the road, and a cast of thousands in her head.

To learn more about Abigail, please visit abigailroux.com.

# Enjoyed this book? Visit RiptidePublishing.com to find more romantic suspense!

*Catch at Ghost*
ISBN: 978-1-62649-039-0

*Santuario*
ISBN: 978-1-937551-65-0

## Earn Bonus Bucks!

Earn 1 Bonus Buck for each dollar you spend. Find out how at RiptidePublishing.com/news/bonus-bucks.

## Win Free Ebooks for a Year!

Pre-order coming soon titles directly through our site and you'll receive one entry into a drawing to win free books for a year! Get the details at RiptidePublishing.com/contests.

Made in the USA
Charleston, SC
31 October 2013